IT TAKES MORE THAN GOOD GRADES TO GRADUATE FROM CENTRAL ACADEMY . . .

Discover the chilling adventures that shadow the halls and stalk the students of **TERROR ACADEMY!**

LIGHTS OUT
School reporter Mandy Roberts investigates the suspicious past of the new assistant principal. The man her widowed mother plans to marry...

STALKER
A tough punk comes back to Central with one requirement to complete: vengeance...

SIXTEEN CANDLES
Kelly Langdon discovers there's more to being popular than she thought—like staying alive...

SPRING BREAK
It's the vacation from hell.
And it's up to Laura Hollister to save her family.
And herself...

THE NEW KID
There's something about the new transfer student.
He's got a deadly secret...

STUDENT BODY
No one's safe at Central—
when a killer roams the halls...

NIGHT SCHOOL
The most handsome teacher in school…
is a vampire!

SCIENCE PROJECT
There's a new formula for terror:
E = mc scared…

THE PROM
It's a party that could raise the dead…

THE IN CROWD
A group of misfits learn a deadly
lesson: if you don't fit in, you may
be out—for good!

SUMMER SCHOOL
Making up is hard to do—when terror is
waiting at summer school…

BREAKING UP
When rich girl meets greaser boy,
love can be a real killer…

THE SUBSTITUTE
Her name is Ms. Green. And her
assignments are murder…

SCHOOL SPIRIT
Are the Central Academy Wildcats sore
losers? Or vicious killers?

For Kim and Heidi Cluff

STUDENT BODY

ONE

Abby Wilder stood at the top of the human pyramid, gazing toward the far, open end of the Central Academy football stadium. From her vantage point, she could see most of the Central campus, including the gymnasium, the dome of the swimming pool building, all three classroom buildings, and the administration offices. She also saw the football team scrimmaging at the other end of the grassy field, which was still green under the mild glow of the October sun.

Abby's stockinged feet rested on the backs of the two girls who formed the tier beneath her on the pyramid. Her arms extended to both sides, parallel to the grass. Abby tried desperately to keep her balance. As the lightest member of the cheerleading squad, Abby was always chosen by Mrs. Seavey to stand at the

1

summit of the living triangle.

Mrs. Mildred Seavey, a chunky brunette woman with a round face, clapped her hands at the ten girls in front of her. "Steady. Come on, you can do better than this. Hold it tight— hold it! Good, keep it up. Don't give in to weakness. We want to look good for the home-coming game."

I just want to go home, Abby thought.

She had never figured that cheerleading could be so hard. The squad's former coach, Miss Edwards, had been fun to work with. Mrs. Seavey was severe and humorless. She always had something nasty to say, even to Abby who was a senior and the squad's captain.

"Steady, Abby," Mrs. Seavey called. "Keep your arms straight!"

Abby sighed and rolled her eyes. Why did Mrs. Seavey always have to pick on her? Abby had been Miss Edward's pet, but Miss Edwards had left Central to move to Colorado and become Mrs. Thompson. Abby wished that Miss Edwards or Mrs. Thompson—whatever she wanted to be called—would move back to Port City to take over the cheerleading squad again.

Mrs. Seavey's pale freckled face frowned disdainfully at Abby, glaring up with pen-etrating green eyes. "Abby, can't you stand any stiller?"

I'm gonna quit, Abby thought. Just like that!

Mrs. Seavey put her hands on her hips and shook her head. "We aren't going to impress anyone like that, girls!"

Abby sighed, focusing her eyes on a boy in a red and white football jersey. He took the ball from the quarterback and turned the corner of the line, racing past the defenders to score a practice touchdown. Abby recognized the number—twenty-four. It was worn by her boyfriend, Billy Major.

"Abby, my goodness, will you stand up straight?"

Abby bit her lip. At five feet four inches and a hundred pounds, she was the only member of the squad who could stand at the top of the pyramid. And she was doing the best she could. Why did Mrs. Seavey always have to slight her performance in front of the others?

Mrs. Seavey exhaled her disgust, pacing back and forth. "Homecoming is only three days away, girls. Don't we want to help our boys win the big game for Central? Root them on to victory."

"Give me a break," Abby muttered under her breath.

Below Abby, on the third row of the pyramid, her best friend Lucy Hale grumbled, "I'd like to break her neck."

"She's going to kill us!" remarked another girl.

"No talking!" Mrs. Seavey snapped.

Abby finally stopped swaying and held steady, freezing in a completely motionless pose atop the pyramid. She watched Billy carry the ball again in the distance. It was a perfect autumn day, except for the woman with the loud mouth who barked orders at them.

"Steady!"

There, Abby thought, smiling, she can't complain now.

But catastrophe lurked around the corner.

Abby felt a wisp of thin blond hair tickling her forehead. She tried to ignore it, but it had come loose from the headband that kept Abby's hair off her face.

"Steady," Mrs. Seavey railed again.

Abby was starting to tremble a bit.

"Abby, what are you—"

It was too late. The strands of hair dropped in front of Abby's nose. Reflexively, Abby focused on the errant strand of golden hair, looking cross-eyed for an instant. She lost her concentration for a single moment, but it was enough to throw her off balance.

"Abby, don't you—"

But Mrs. Seavey's snarling tone could not stop Abby from falling and taking the pyramid down with her. Ten girls in white sweat suits tumbled onto the thick carpet of grass, rolling in every direction, dazed but unhurt.

The fallen girls sprawled on the grass, seizing the moment to rest from the rigors of Mrs. Seavey's cheerleading drills. Abby immediately began to giggle. She couldn't help herself. The whole thing seemed so ridiculous.

"Stop that!" Mrs. Seavey bellowed. "This is no laughing matter. Do you hear me?"

But Abby's giggle had already transformed into a full-fledged burst of laughter. Mrs. Seavey towered over her, blocking Abby's view of the clear blue sky. Abby wanted to stop, but she couldn't. She had a terrible case of the uncontrollable chuckles.

"It's not funny!" Mrs. Seavey cried.

Lucy started to laugh with Abby. Mrs. Seavey swung in her direction, glaring at the tall, athletic girl with short black hair. Despite Mrs. Seavey's stern warnings, Lucy began to roll around on the grass, giggling like a third-grader.

"Stop it now!" Mrs. Seavey went on. "I mean it! I'll cancel your appearance at the homecoming game."

But the threats weren't working. Abby's laughter had become infectious. All of the girls started to laugh, releasing the nervous tension. The more Mrs. Seavey hollered at them, the more inclined they were to giggle.

Abby stopped suddenly and sat up straight. She knew she was going to get blamed for the chaos that had descended on the group. Mrs. Seavey tended to blame Abby for everything.

Sure enough, the chunky woman turned toward Abby, scowling like a demon. "You're the cause of all this! As the captain of the squad, you're supposed to set an example for the others."

Abby opened her mouth to speak but nothing came out. She was speechless. She didn't know what to say to Mrs. Seavey.

"You had better change your tune, young lady," Mrs. Seavey said. "If you don't shape up, you can count on—"

"Aw, lighten up, bubble-butt!"

Mrs. Seavey stiffened. Her face turned bright red. Abby thought that steam or blood might start to come out of Mrs. Seavey's ears.

The thick woman turned in a slow circle. "Who said that?"

Abby was frozen on the cool ground. She knew who had made the rude comment. She recognized Lucy's voice. Abby had heard it almost every day since the fourth grade. She wondered if Mrs. Seavey recognized it.

Mrs. Seavey's green eyes were bulging. "Who said it?"

"Said what?" Abby chimed in. "I didn't hear anything."

The teacher wheeled in Abby's direction again. "Was it you?"

Abby shrugged nonchalantly. "You were looking right at me, Mrs. Seavey," she said innocently. "I didn't say anything."

"Then who said it?"

"Said what?" Lucy rejoined. "I didn't hear a thing."

Another girl came to Lucy's defense. "No, I didn't hear anything either."

The chorus grew around the group.

"Hear what?"

"I didn't hear anything."

"Did you hear anything?"

Mrs. Seavey was not about to repeat the slur, so she could only fume with her hands on her hips. "Do you girls know how lucky you are to be cheerleaders?"

Abby jumped quickly to her feet. "I don't care, Mrs. Seavey. I'm quitting!"

Mrs. Seavey's jaw dropped. "What?"

Lucy stood as well. "Me too. I've had it. I'm out of here."

The other girls joined in the show of solidarity. They all vowed to quit the squad with Abby and Lucy. Mrs. Seavey watched as they started to walk away from her.

"Wait!" she said, her voice urgent. "I— I'm sorry, I didn't mean to . . . that is . . . please . . . I'm sorry."

The girls had turned their backs on Mrs. Seavey. Abby glanced sideways at Lucy. Her best friend's eyes glinted with a knowing, impish expression. Lucy winked at her. They both knew they had Mrs. Seavey over a barrel. If the whole cheerleading squad quit on her, Mrs. Seavey would look bad in the eyes of the rest of the Central faculty and administration.

"Please, girls, I'm sorry. All right?"

Abby spun around, her blue eyes glaring, hands resting on her slender hips. She didn't reply immediately; Abby wanted Mrs. Seavey to know who held the upper hand.

The other cheerleaders gathered behind Abby, showing their support. No one really wanted to quit, but they knew they had to stand up to their slave-driving coach.

Mrs. Seavey took a deep breath, trying to compose herself. "All right, let's calm down. I know we've had a tough time, but there's no reason to fly off the—"

Abby spoke up, interrupting her. "There's no reason for us to stay on the squad, not if you're going to treat us like garbage."

The others nodded and muttered in agreement.

Mrs. Seavey stiffened, her face tensing for a moment. She looked like she was going to explode. The girls had seen her temper before.

She was always venting her anger on them.

But Abby no longer cared. Mrs. Seavey didn't frighten her now. She removed her elastic headband and shook her head, allowing her mane of blond hair to fall around her shoulders. Her full, coral lips were set firmly in a defiant pout. Abby was beautiful, spoiled, and used to getting her own way in life.

Mrs. Seavey seemed to deflate. "I haven't treated anyone like garbage—"

Abby snorted derisively. "Yes you have!"

"I just want you to be the best," the older woman pleaded. "I just—"

The whole cheerleading squad groaned in unison.

Abby sure wasn't buying the innocent act. "You enjoy being rotten to us, Mrs. Seavey. Admit it."

"No, believe me, I—"

"Then why do you yell at us all the time?" Abby challenged. "Nothing we do is ever good enough for you."

"But I—"

Lucy gazed over Abby's shoulder. "Yeah, we don't care about being the best. We just want to have fun, like we did with Miss Edwards."

Mrs. Seavey's brow wrinkled with anger. "I'm not Miss Edwards."

"For sure," Abby replied. "She was nice.

You're like some . . . I don't know . . . some bogus Nazi or something."

Mrs. Seavey waved at them. "Go on, quit. See if I care. I can have another squad of girls ready by homecoming."

Abby smirked and waved her pinky finger. "Fine. See ya."

As Abby turned again, the rest of the girls turned with her. It had all happened so quickly. Abby's stomach was churning. She hoped that Mrs. Seavey would buy the bluff. She was a new teacher at Central, so she wanted to make a good impression. She had to buckle under—she just had to!

Lucy spoke from the corner of her mouth. "Abby, what if she really lets us quit the squad?"

Abby had crossed her fingers. "She can't have a squad ready by homecoming. It's impossible."

"Yeah," one of the other girls replied, "we're the best. She can't replace us in three days."

I hope not, Abby thought.

"Wait!" Mrs. Seavey cried.

Abby stopped in her tracks. "I told you so."

Lucy grinned. "I still hate her."

Abby spun back to meet Mrs. Seavey's pitiful gaze. She almost felt sorry for the red-faced widow. Everyone knew that Mrs. Seavey had lost her husband a couple of years earlier.

Maybe she was really just a soft ball of mush inside. The girls had made her crumble by standing up to her.

Mrs. Seavey sighed. "All right, what do you want me to do?"

Abby had been thinking about what she would say to Mrs. Seavey, had imagined this moment for an entire month. Now that it was here, she had to make the most of it.

"Tell her," Lucy muttered.

All of the girls were depending on Abby. She couldn't let them down. The fate of the Central Academy cheerleading squad was in her hands.

"I'm waiting," Mrs. Seavey said.

Abby took a deep breath. "First, you can cut back the practices from three hours to two."

Mrs. Seavey grimaced at the idea, but she nodded her head anyway. "Okay, I can live with that."

Abby began to gain more confidence. "We want to do some of the cheers we did last year. The ones we learned under Miss Edwards. I mean, some of us have been doing those cheers for three years."

"The same old cheers?" Mrs. Seavey asked. "But—"

"Not all of them, just some," Abby said. "Everyone at Central likes those same old cheers."

"Yeah," Lucy interjected. "They like them."

One by one, Mrs. Seavey looked into the faces of the other girls. They stood their ground.

"We want it to be fun again," Abby went on. "We don't like doing all this acrobatic stuff. Oh, some of it is okay, but we hate the pyramid. I mean, we're cheerleaders, not circus performers."

Mrs. Seavey nodded. "All right. Have it your way. No more pyramid. And practices will be two hours."

"Three days a week." Abby challenged.

Mrs. Seavey grimaced again. "Three days?"

"And no weekends," Abby said. "Otherwise we walk."

"But the state cheer-off," Mrs. Seavey pleaded. "We won't win if we don't make some kind of commitment."

Abby rolled her eyes. "We have lives, Mrs. Seavey. We have to study. We like to go out on dates. Some of us are going to take our SAT's this year. I mean, we all love to cheer, but enough is enough."

Moisture was gathering at the corners of Mrs. Seavey's green eyes. A single tear fell onto her cheek, sliding down her chubby face. She was actually starting to cry in front of them.

Abby almost felt sorry for her. Some of the

other girls were having second thoughts about standing up to her. The ogre had suddenly turned into a real person with emotions.

"Don't buy it," Lucy whispered. "It's an act."

"I just wanted you to win that cheer-off," Mrs. Seavey offered.

Abby didn't really believe the act either. "I'm sorry, Mrs. Seavey, but we aren't backing off. You agree to shorten the practices and lay off all the yelling and acrobatics. That's it. Take it or leave it."

Mrs. Seavey threw out her hands. "You win. The cheer-offs aren't until spring anyway. If you still want to apply yourselves then . . ."

"We want to have fun," Abby replied.

"Very well. I'll see you tomorrow—I mean, Thursday."

Mrs. Seavey turned away, walking quickly toward the gymnasium in the distance. Her head was hanging low as she left them. Abby felt badly for a moment, but then the other girls circled around her, patting her on the back and laughing.

"You did it, Abby!"

"That was great!"

"Nice moves, Wilder," Lucy said.

Abby smiled. "Okay, okay, I got the monster off our backs. Let's go for some pizza. My treat."

They all cheered their new liberator. Abby

could afford to buy pizza and sodas. She got a generous allowance from her rich father.

"I'll meet you at Pizza Palace in the mall," Abby said.

Everyone rushed toward the gym except Lucy.

"Wow, Abby, you really stood up to her."

Abby sighed. "I feel kind of bad about it."

Lucy nodded toward the lone boy who walked toward them in a football uniform. "Here comes someone who ought to make you feel better."

It was Billy Major, the star running back for the Central Academy football team. Practice was over for everyone now. Billy was looking straight at Abby as he approached.

Abby bit her lip. Billy didn't look happy. And she knew exactly why her boyfriend was in bad spirits.

TWO

Billy Major, who stood six feet two inches
and weighed a hundred and eighty-five
nds, looked like a behemoth in his foot-
uniform. His brown hair was plastered
his forehead by perspiration, his hand-
ne face glowing red after a rough scrim-
hage. Stopping a few feet away from Abby
and Lucy, he held the red and white football helmet by the face mask, squinting at
he girls with an impatient gleam in his
brown eyes.

Abby shivered at Billy's accusing expression. He was easily the best looking boy
at Central Academy. All the girls, includ-
ng Lucy, were envious of Abby for going
eady with the team captain, the gridiron
ero, the most popular boy in school. Abby

had been going with Billy for over a year, but lately things had been strained between them.

Lucy squinted at Billy. "What's his problem?" she said in a whisper.

"Later," Abby replied, trying to smile. "Hi, Billy."

Billy grunted and shifted his helmet to the other hand. "Yeah, hi. Practice is over."

Lucy offered a pleasant, "Hello, Billy."

He scowled at her, the belligerent jock. "Hey, Lucy, don't you have someplace else to go?"

Lucy shrugged, taking the hint. "Uh, I gu
See you at the mall, Abs." She turned to
away.

Abby grabbed her arm. "No, stay with
We have to meet the other girls at the ma
Billy. I can't talk right now."

Billy shook his head, smirking at them. "I
thought we were going to talk some more,
about, well, you know. . . ."

Abby's pretty face twisted into a look of
impatience. "Billy, this isn't the time or place
to talk about *that*."

"When?" he asked.

Lucy shifted nervously on the balls of h
feet. "Maybe I should just—"

Billy grimaced at her. "Yeah, maybe yo
should."

Abby met Billy's impudence with a willful assertion of her own. "Maybe you should just call me tonight, Billy. That would be better for both of us."

He nodded, smiling a little, his voice taking on a more friendly tone. "Maybe I'll come by—if that's okay."

"Sure," Abby replied. "Uh, my mom and dad will be home."

Billy chortled, gazing off into the distance. "Yeah, I should've known that."

Abby wanted to be understanding, but it was tough with Billy acting like such a creep. "Don't be that way."

He pointed at her with the football helmet. "How do you want me to be?"

Lucy blushed, wishing that she wasn't in the middle of a spat between boyfriend and girlfriend. She had a boyfriend of her own, Jimmy Clayton, who was on the basketball team. Jimmy wasn't anywhere near as moody or as demanding as Billy.

"Just call me," Abby said. "We'll talk."

"You're *all* talk," Billy replied. "I'm tired of talking, Abby. I've had it."

She stiffened, attempting to maintain her dignity. "Then tough! Do you want your ring back? I'll be happy to—"

He wheeled away from them, heading for

the boy's locker room under the stadium. "I'm outta here."

Abby fought the urge to cry. The tears were there, but she refused to give in. It had been a trying day, first standing up to Mrs. Seavey and now this.

Lucy shook her head, watching Billy as he swaggered across the field. "What was that all about?"

"He wants something that I'm not ready to give him," Abby replied. "Not yet."

"What?" Lucy asked.

Abby sighed. "What do boys always want?"

"Oohh, I see. So why don't you just tell him you want to wait a little longer?"

"I did," Abby replied. "That's what all the hassle is about."

Lucy sighed. "Boys."

Abby shook her head. "I'm afraid I'm going to lose him if I don't give in."

Lucy looked at her best friend with dismay. "Do you love him?" she asked.

Abby sighed deeply. "I don't know. I used to think I did but lately everything I do has to be for him. He doesn't care what I want or what I think."

"Boys *again*! Come on, let's change and get to the mall."

Abby turned back toward the section of the field where the squad had been practicing.

"Look. Everyone forgot their pom-poms. They were so excited about standing up to Mrs. Seavey."

"I'll help you," Lucy said.

Abby waved her toward the gym. "Go on, I'll be able to carry them. They're only pom-poms."

Lucy studied Abby, wondering if Abby was really depressed or just a little blue. "Are you gonna be okay, Abs?"

"Yeah, I just want a minute alone. I'll be fine."

Lucy started off in the direction of the gym.

Abby went toward the pile of red and white pom-poms. She was thinking about Billy and the demands he was making on her. It didn't help to know that every girl had to make the same decision sooner or later. If she was this uncertain, didn't that mean she *wasn't* ready for such a big step?

She bent down to pick up her set of pom-poms. If she gave in, the worst might happen. Billy said he was experienced in such matters, but Abby figured he was just blowing smoke.

"Hi, Abby, how ya doing?"

She turned to her left to see a short, skinny boy coming toward her. Abby grimaced. It was Frankie Deets, the manager of the football team. Frankie had a crew cut and a mousy face. He was a typical wannabe, always trying to hang out with the popular kids.

"Help you with those pom-poms?" Frankie asked, though he was eyeing Abby up and down.

"I can do it, Frankie."

But he was determined to help her, moving closer, trying to brush against her as he picked up the fluffy balls of red and white crepe paper. "Lookin' pretty good out there today, Abby."

She just ignored him.

Frankie could never take a hint. "I saw the way Billy was treating you."

Her eyes narrowed. "What business is that of yours?"

He shrugged. "I dunno. I just thought, well, if I had a girlfriend like you, I wouldn't treat her bad."

"Get real," Abby replied in a hostile tone.

Frankie still didn't get the message. "Yeah, Billy is the luckiest kid in the school to be going out with an ultra-stone fox like you, Abby. He doesn't know how good he has it."

Abby had just about taken enough from this fresh sophomore. "I'm going to tell him you said that, Frankie."

Frankie's lower lip began to tremble. His grayish eyes flickered back and forth like he was looking for Billy. Billy could tear Frankie apart, and Frankie knew it.

"Uh, I didn't mean anything, Abby," he said softly.

"Then keep your mouth shut," Abby replied.

By this time, their arms were full of the pom-poms. They started walking back to the gym. Frankie had to walk fast to keep up with Abby's long-legged strides. She was at least a head taller than him.

"Uh, Abby," Frankie went on. "I was wonderin' if you had a date for homecoming."

Abby stopped dead in her tracks. Frankie couldn't be serious. Was he really going to ask her to the dance? After all, Abby could've been homecoming queen, had she not chosen to forgo the homecoming court so she could cheer during the big game.

Frankie came up beside her, smiling. "Because, if you aren't going with Billy, I'd be happy to—"

Abby didn't hear the rest. Her face had turned red. What was this anyway? Dweeb sympathy day?

"What'll it be, Abby? Do you want to—"

His voice became muffled as Abby did something really mean and hostile.

"So what'd you do?" Lucy asked, looking over the slice of pepperoni pizza as she lifted it toward her mouth.

Abby was half-smiling at her retelling of the incident with Frankie Deets. "I dumped all the pom-poms on him," she said.

Lucy and the four other girls broke into guffaws. Abby felt better than she had after cheerleading practice. Sometimes she got a great deal of pleasure from humiliating the school nerds. It was one of the privileges that came with popularity.

Abby tossed her mane of blond hair and her lips curved in a haughty smile. "He's a dwarf. A cockroach. A munchkin. I'd quit school before I'd go to the homecoming dance with that little geek."

The other girls were laughing so hard they almost choked on their pizza. Abby had a way of being the center of attention; she wouldn't settle for anything less.

"Can you imagine dancing with him?" she went on. "He'd have his face in your—"

Her eyes dipped downward.

Lucy wiped the tears of laughter from her eyes. "It's be great, just great."

"For *him*!" Abby cried indignantly.

They broke up again, almost spilling their sodas.

Abby often took members of the squad to the Pizza Palace in Tremont Mall. She didn't have to pick up the check every time, but she always did. Despite her good looks, intelligence, and

immense popularity, Abby still had an overwhelming need to be liked, to be the life of
the party.

Her face tightened as she watched the other
girls. Lately, she had begun to wonder if it was
all worth it. It took a great deal of energy to
be a celebrity at Central. She was involved in
cheering, was managing editor of the yearbook
staff, served as vice president of the student
council. Everyone wanted to be like her. The
boys wanted to take her out, the girls wished
they were her. She had it made—in everyone
else's eyes.

"What a shrimp!" Lucy said. "Can you imagine Frankie and Abby as a couple?"

Abby felt a sudden pang of remorse about
the way she had treated Frankie. After all, he
was a human being. He had hopes and dreams
like everyone else. What right did she really
have to be so mean to him, even if he was a
dweeb?

But her better nature was quickly lost in
the chorus of laughter from her friends.

"I could be bridesmaid at the wedding," Lucy
went on. "Do you, Abby, take this troll to be
your lawfully wedded geek-boy?"

"I now pronounce you wife and twerp."

They were still giggling when the waitress
brought the check. Abby paid with a fifty-
dollar bill. Her father was a big lawyer in

Port City. They lived in Prescott Estates, the fanciest neighborhood in the quaint, seaside, New England community. The Wilders were one of the most respected and envied families in town.

"Anybody need a ride home?" Abby asked as they were rising from the table.

Abby always drove too. She had a new Chrysler minivan that her mother and father had given her for her seventeenth birthday the month before.

Everyone wanted to be Abby . . . but Abby wasn't so sure she wanted to be herself.

The five girls hurried through the mall, emerging into the parking lot. They piled into Abby's van. She could've had a car that was more sporty and stylish, but she chose the van so she could carry all of her friends around.

They drove along Middle Road, following the route of the Tide Gate River that flowed out to the Atlantic Ocean. The town was alive with the bright reds, yellows, and oranges of autumn. Ears of Indian corn adorned the front doors of houses that would soon have smiling jack-o'-lanterns in the windows and on the stoops. It was the perfect fall setting for a homecoming game and dance.

Why then, Abby wondered, was she feeling so depressed about everything?

They dropped off the first girl, Alice, in the middle of town because she wanted to stop at a record store. The next rider, Susan, lived in Morningside Groves, a new development of small ranch-style houses. They had to go out to Hampton Way Beach to drop off Trudy, a muscular red-haired junior who had only made the cheerleading squad this year.

Lucy said, "Don't you ever get tired of playing taxi driver?"

Abby shrugged. "No, not really. They're all good kids. Aren't they? I mean, they backed me up with Mrs. Seavey." She sighed.

Lucy squinted at her. "What's wrong? Is it Billy?"

Abby nodded. "I guess."

"Tell him to jump in the river," Lucy replied. "Who cares if you lose him?"

Abby just nodded, guiding the van back toward town on Beach Road. Lucy also lived in Prescott Estates, a few blocks away from Abby.

"Want me to drop you off?" Abby asked.

"Nah," Lucy said. "Mind if I come over? We can tackle that Latin translation together and study for tomorrow's quiz."

"Latin," Abby said absently, "Why did I ever sign up for a dead language?"

"Because," Lucy replied like she was reciting

a course catalog, "Central Academy is dedicated to preparing students for college work and a life of intellectual—"

"Can it, Hale. I don't need it."

"*Et tu*, Wilder."

They laughed like silly children. Abby drove back through town, passing Old North Church and Town Hall. When they went by Old Cemetery, she remembered how she and Lucy used to sneak out at night to run between the gravestones. They had been ten or eleven years old the first time they made a midnight run.

"I'm scared, Lucy," Abby said suddenly.

Lucy did not reply. She knew how Abby was feeling. Lucy had lost one boyfriend because she had not given in to temptation.

The van entered Prescott Estates, passing the twin pillars that marked the gates of the fancy neighborhood. Abby was oblivious to the autumn grandeur that colored the mixture of new and classic colonial structures. She was thinking about other things. And it wasn't about to get any better.

"Look," Lucy said, pointing toward Abby's two-story house.

"Oh no," Abby groaned.

Parked in front of her house was a red Toyota Camry. A boy leaned against the front fender, his arms folded over his chest. Even in the dim light of afternoon, Abby was aware that Billy had shown up to pressure her.

And he knew by the empty driveway that her parents weren't home.

THREE

Abby bit her lip as she guided the van into the driveway. She wasn't ready for Billy, not now. Not with her parents gone from the huge white house. She didn't want to be alone with Billy. A creepy feeling had come over her every time she thought about his demanding nature. She didn't like being pressured into anything.

Billy glared at her with narrow-eyed intensity, leaning on his car. His arms were folded, his head tilted in an arrogant, jock angle. What had happened to the sweet guy she had dated as a junior? she wondered. Billy had changed a lot during their senior year.

Abby got out of the van. Lucy hesitated before she stepped into the driveway. Billy glowered at her from the street. He had hoped

29

that Abby would be alone. Lucy's presence was a disappointment.

Lucy turned to Abby, who was walking around in front of the van. "Want me to leave? I could walk home."

Abby came up next to her. "No! I don't want to be alone with him."

Lucy grimaced, watching as Billy slid off the Toyota. "What happened to him?"

Billy started to walk toward them, strutting.

Abby sighed and shook her head. "I don't know. Maybe it's the football team. He's the big star now. Last year he didn't get to play as much."

Billy strode up to them and scowled at Lucy. "Are you gonna be hanging around, Lucy?"

Lucy started to speak, but Abby cut in.

"Billy, we're going to study," she said to her boyfriend.

Billy shrugged, then smiled. "I could get into that."

Abby bit her lip again. "Really?"

"Sure," he replied. "I'll get my notebook."

He started back toward the car.

Abby frowned. "That's a switch. He never wants to study."

Lucy was blushing a little. "Maybe I should take off, Abs. I mean, you guys have an awful lot to talk about—"

Abby grabbed her arm. "You're staying. I don't trust him lately. He's been too—too eager."

"Okay," Lucy replied. "But if you want me to leave, just say so. My feelings won't be hurt."

Billy reached into his car and pulled out a looseleaf binder. He came back toward them, grinning. Abby was almost certain that he had no intention of studying. But she was willing to give him the benefit of a slender doubt.

"Let's crack the books," Billy said glibly.

Abby led them into the spacious, meticulously decorated living room of the Wilder house. Her mother would settle for only the best furniture and accessories. Abby liked living in a nice place, though some of her less well-off friends were intimidated by the ornate palace that Abby called home.

Lucy sunk down on a plush sofa. "Wow, I need a rest. I'm sore after practice."

Billy leered at her. "So am I. Maybe I'll go upstairs and take a quick nap. Anybody want to join me?"

Abby tensed and frowned at him. "Billy, if you're going to start this kind of—"

Billy said, "Relax, Abster. I was only making a joke."

He plopped into an easy chair.

Abby's disapproving eyes lingered on him for a moment. She wanted to throw him out.

He was acting like such a dweeb. Worse than Frankie Deets!

Billy actually opened his notebook and started to read something.

Lucy shifted nervously on the sofa. She didn't want to be caught in the middle of anything. She could feel the tension between them, thicker than a sheet of ice.

"Maybe I should go," she offered.

Abby turned to glare at her, mouthing the word, *No!*

Billy's eyes lifted from the notebook. "Well, if you gotta go, Lucy—"

"She's staying," Abby insisted.

Billy rolled his eyes toward the ceiling. "Great. Just great. I thought we might have a chance to talk a little."

But Abby wasn't buying into Billy's offer. "We have to study. That's more important."

Billy exhaled. "Well, hey, will one of you wenches get me something to drink?"

Lucy gawked at him. "Billy, you're so obnoxious."

He pointed at her. "Yeah, well, a motorcycle doesn't need three wheels to glide, Lucy. And that's just what you are! A third wheel."

Abby stepped in front of Billy. "That's enough."

He gestured at Lucy again. "Oh yeah, defend *her*! I've only been your boyfriend for a year."

"Then act like my boyfriend," Abby replied.
"Show me a little respect."

Billy slumped in the chair. "All I want is
something to drink. A soda or something. I'll
get it myself."

Abby took a deep breath and exhaled. "No,
I'll get something for all of us. Wait here."

She exited the living room, heading down
the hall to the kitchen. Abby was tired and
confused. She really didn't feel like dealing
with Billy, not today. It made her sad to think
that the relationship was probably over. But
Billy hadn't given her much to cling to, not
with his overbearing routine.

"Darn!"

The refrigerator was almost empty. Her
mother was no doubt shopping. Abby would
have to go down into the cellar to get some diet
soda. She opened the cellar door and flipped
on the light. Tiptoeing down the steep, narrow
staircase, she descended into the cool air of the
basement.

The cramped, dank enclosure had frightened
Abby as a child. She and Lucy had played a
game they called "Monsters" in the shadows of
the cellar, scaring each other until they were
too old to be afraid of such nonsense. Now
Abby went down into the basement without
any fears of ghosts and goblins.

Reaching high on a shelf, she found a two-liter bottle of diet soda. Abby had to dust off the top of the bottle. She turned back toward the steps, maneuvering through the dim light. For a moment, she felt a chill on the back of her neck, like something cold had touched her. But it seemed to be nothing more than a draft that disappeared as soon as she began to walk up the stairs.

When she arrived at the top of the staircase, she flipped off the basement light and turned to step into the kitchen. Abby suddenly realized that the kitchen was now dark. The fading glow of the sun had left Port City in nightfall.

Abby shivered at another cold touch on her neck. She remembered leaving the light on in the kitchen. Who had turned it off?

As she lifted her hand toward the switch on the wall, someone grabbed her wrist. Abby struggled for a moment, dropping the bottle of soda. The intruder threw her back against the closed basement door, trapping her there.

"I thought we'd never be alone," Billy whispered.

Abby stopped struggling, though she did not relax. "Get off me, Billy!"

Billy lowered his mouth toward her face, trying to kiss her.

Abby shook her head back and forth, avoiding his lips. She was ready to scream if he didn't stop. Lucy was in the next room and would come to her aid, if necessary.

"You let me kiss you before!" Billy insisted.

Abby glared at him. "That was when you were being nice to me. I used to like you."

Billy would not give up. "You still like me. Come on, one kiss. What's it gonna hurt?"

"No, Billy."

"You're going to kiss me!" he said through clenched teeth.

He came at her again.

"I'm going to scream, Billy."

He pressed his mouth against her ear. "No you won't. You love it, babe."

"Lucy!"

Abby's cry echoed through the house.

Billy grimaced and started to step back. "You little—"

When she felt him moving away from her, Abby lifted her knee, nailing Billy right in the groin. He doubled over just as Lucy rushed into the dark kitchen. Billy hit the floor on one knee, groaning pitifully.

Lucy switched on the overhead light. "What happened?"

Billy fell onto his side. "She kicked me!"

Abby shuddered. "He had it coming. He ambushed me in the dark. He could have been a gentleman, but no!"

Lucy shook her head. "I knew he was coming in here to cause trouble. Boy, you really decked him."

Abby was weak-kneed. She wasn't proud of what she had done to Billy. Mrs. Seavey had instructed all the girls in self-defense at the beginning of the year, a precaution that had paid off. At least the old battle-ax had taught her something.

"It hurts," Billy groaned.

Lucy gaped at him. "I hope you haven't ruined him for the big homecoming game."

Abby picked up the soda bottle that she had dropped when Billy jumped from the shadows. "I had to do it, Lucy. Who knows what he would have tried if I hadn't."

"Just wanted a kiss," Billy muttered through the pain.

Abby shook her head, exhaling. "Come on, let's take him to his car."

"I'll have to drive him home," Lucy said. "He's in no shape to get behind the wheel."

Abby bent to help him from the floor. Lucy also lent a hand. They raised him up on wobbly legs. With their assistance, he was able to make it to the Toyota.

"I'm gonna fix you, Abby," he said with a strained voice. "I mean it."

Billy flopped into the passenger seat of his own car, leaning back his head. Abby was sorry that she had hurt him. But she knew that

she had avoided a much worse fate herself.
Billy had to be taught a lesson and she had
delivered it with force.

"Gonna fix you," he repeated.

Lucy made a face. "Wow, he's really out of
it. How hard did you hit him?"

"Just take him home," Abby replied. "He'll
get over it."

The shadows were thickening in Port City.
Porch lights had begun to glow in Prescott
Estates. Lucy said good night and climbed
behind the wheel of the Toyota.

Abby watched as the red taillights disappeared around the corner. She was spent,
numb, on the verge of tears. Even Central's
most popular member of the student body had
bad days. She turned and hurried back into
the house.

Abby grabbed her books from the living
room and went upstairs. Her own bedroom
was done up in lavender and white, complete
with a canopy bed covered with stuffed toys. It
was the chamber of a spoiled rich girl, bright
and cheery, as if the inhabitant had not one
single care in the world.

But Abby had a multitude of worries as
she lay down on her soft comforter. She tried
to study, but couldn't concentrate. She kept
thinking about Billy, how their relationship
had turned so sour in the short time since

the beginning of school. Was there any way to
save their relationship? Abby thought it was
pretty hopeless, especially after the incident
in the kitchen.

A car horn honked in the driveway. Her
mother was home. Abby suddenly felt the
overwhelming need to talk to her mother, to
ask her advice about Billy. Climbing off the
bed, she ran down to help her mother carry
in the groceries.

Teri Wilder was a handsome woman, tall and
blond like her daughter. She worked as an interior decorating consultant, ranging from Port
City all the way north to Burlington in her
travels. Like Abby's father, who often worked
until midnight, Teri Wilder was away from
home a lot.

"Hi, Mom," Abby said cheerfully.

Mrs. Wilder only grunted and handed her
a bag of groceries. "I'm going to have to teach
you to do the shopping."

Abby sighed. "Sure, Mom, whatever."

They unloaded Mrs. Wilder's red Subaru
wagon, carrying four bags into the kitchen.
Abby kept watching her mother, hoping to
talk. But Mrs. Wilder seemed distracted.

"Mom?"

"What?" Mrs. Wilder snapped impatiently.

"Uh . . . I just wanted to talk to you about
something."

Mrs. Wilder glared at her daughter. "Can't it wait, Abby? I've had a hideous day. Don't you have homework or something?"

Abby felt the tears welling in the corners of her eyes. "Sure, Mom. Later."

She ran back to her room, dropping on the bed. She cried until the phone rang. It was Lucy with a report on her drive to Billy's.

"He acted like he was dying," Lucy said. "I thought he was going to barf once. But he seemed to be better after I got him home."

Abby sniffed wetly, not replying.

"Are you all right?" Lucy asked.

Abby took a deep breath and sighed. "I don't know what to do about Billy."

Lucy hesitated, then replied, "Blow him off, Abs. Break it off before—"

"Before what?" Abby asked, fearing the answer with butterflies fluttering in her stomach.

Lucy searched for the right words. "Well, all the way home he kept saying that he, uh . . . well . . . he—"

"Just say it," Abby demanded.

"He's going to ask for his ring back," Lucy replied quickly.

Abby waited for the intense pain, but it never came. Instead, she experienced a sensation of relief. There was some sadness inside her, but it wasn't overwhelming.

"Abs, are you there?"

"Yes," Abby replied. "And don't worry. He'll get his ring back. With pleasure."

It was Lucy's turn to sigh. "I'm sorry, Abs."

A numbness settled over Abby, but it was better than pain. She felt sleepy all of a sudden, with a need to put the horrible day behind her.

"I'm beat," she told Lucy. "I'm going to crash for the rest of the night."

"I could come over," Lucy offered.

"No. I'll see you tomorrow."

"Call me if you need to talk, Abs."

"I will."

Abby said good-bye and hung up.

The phone rang immediately. It was Abby's private line, so she had to answer. Her nerves tingled again at the thought of talking to Billy. It wasn't a good feeling.

"Hello, Abby, this is Mrs. Seavey."

Abby was silent, wondering if the cheerleading coach had called her up to be nasty about what had happened earlier that day.

"I'm sorry to bother you," she went on, "but I just wanted to make sure that you understand that there are no hard feelings on my part. About that little squabble, I mean."

Abby wasn't sure what to think. Mrs. Seavey had never called her at home before. It was sort of weird, hearing her voice on the phone.

"Uh, it's okay," Abby replied. "I'm sorry too."

Mrs. Seavey virtually cooed, "Oh, Abby, you're so talented. You could really lead the squad to a championship in the cheer-off this spring. If you could just work with me. . . . Well, I just want you to know that we could win the cheer-off with your help."

Abby knew she was being manipulated, but that didn't stop her from letting her ego reap the rewards of praise. "Uh, I'll do my best, Mrs. Seavey."

"Thank you so much, Abby. We'll talk at the next practice. Okay with you?"

"Yes, Mrs. Seavey. Good night."

Abby hung up. It had certainly been a strange day. And it quickly got stranger. Again the phone rang, bringing a familiar, hostile voice right into her room.

"You're gonna get it!" Billy railed. "You'll see. I'm going to fix you good."

Abby's temper swelled and her face grew red. "We're through, Billy. You can have your ring back anytime."

She slammed down the receiver, her hands trembling. She started to cry. No way could things get any worse, she thought.

She was wrong.

FOUR

When Abby awakened the next morning, she felt better, but by no means joyous. She still had to face the day at Central Academy. Everyone would hear about the breakup sooner or later. It would be the juicy gossip in all the hallways. Abby and Billy were quits, *fini*, splitsville, history. And Billy would no doubt be telling everyone that *he* broke up with Abby first.

Abby took a shower, fixed her hair, and dressed in a pair of black jeans and a black sweater. It was almost like she was in mourning for her dead relationship.

Her parents had already left by the time she got to the kitchen, so she made her own breakfast. There was a note from her mother that both of her parents would be late. Mrs. Wilder had left money with the note, one hundred dollars. It was understood that Abby would buy her own lunch and dinner too.

Abby sighed, gazing down at the green bills in her fingers. She hadn't even seen her father in a couple of days. How many kids would have welcomed a hundred dollars? It meant nothing to Abby.

She ate a cup of yogurt and a banana. She was running late, so she grabbed her books and hurried out. It was another lovely fall day, slightly brisk with the sun reflecting gold and crimson off the changing trees.

The minivan rolled through Prescott Estates. She picked up Lucy, who smiled and tried to be friendly. When Abby did not respond, Lucy eventually grew quiet.

"Everyone will know about me and Billy," Abby said finally.

Lucy glanced sideways at her. "Not because they heard it from me," she said defensively.

Abby's face tightened. "I know. But they'll still hear."

"Forget it," Lucy replied. "Breakups happen all the time. It won't be the first."

Abby had broken off with boys before, but somehow this felt different. Billy had been so creepy to her lately. She wondered if he would lose it if they really called it quits. Sometimes boys could be obsessive after being dumped. Did she have anything to fear from Billy?

"Are you okay?" Lucy asked.

Abby nodded. "I'm a little scared."

"Really?"

"Billy has been really strange this year. I mean, he was getting rough last night."

"Just tell him to stay away from you," Lucy replied. "Besides, when everyone finds out he's free, all the girls will be lining up to go out with him."

Abby gave her an incredulous look. "Thanks!"

Lucy's face flushed red. "I'm sorry, that came out wrong—"

Abby focused her eyes on Middle Road. As she turned in the direction of Central Academy, Abby quickly realized that she didn't much care who got Billy after they said goodbye. It might be wise to warn his new girlfriend about Billy's less-than-honorable intentions. Of course, there were girls, even at Central, who had no problem with it.

Lucy pointed to the figure of a young man ahead of them on Middle Road. "Look, it's Frankie."

Frankie Deets, the football manager, was walking rapidly along Middle Road.

Abby sighed. "He lives all the way out at Rye. I bet he missed his bus and had to walk. I think I'll give him a ride."

Lucy gaped at her. "No way."

"I feel guilty about dumping those pom-poms on him."

"Abby!"

But it was too late. Abby's better nature had won out. She pulled over and let Frankie into the back of the minivan.

Frankie jumped in, sweating and out of breath. "Thanks, Abby," he said, gazing at her in adoration. He couldn't believe his luck.

They rolled toward Central with Lucy glaring daggers at her best friend. Abby just shrugged. For some reason, she was feeling generous, though her largesse quickly dissolved with Frankie's next statement.

"Sorry to hear Billy broke off with you," Frankie whined.

Abby glanced at him in her rearview mirror. "How'd you know about that, Frankie?"

Frankie leaned forward and Abby could smell his bad breath. "Billy called me up to tell me."

Lucy glared at Frankie. "Billy called *you*?"

Frankie shrugged. He had been surprised when Billy called him. He hadn't figured he was that important to anyone, especially Billy.

"Oh no," Lucy moaned. "If Billy called Frankie, then he must've been calling everyone."

Frankie blushed and leaned back, taking his rat-breath with him. "He said he called every-

one. The whole school will know by the time
we get there. It's no secret."

Lucy looked worriedly at her best friend.
"Abs, are you going to be all right?"

Abby bit her lip and tightened her hold on
the steering wheel. Maybe it was better that
everyone already knew. That way she wouldn't
have to field a bunch of dumb questions.

She couldn't help but worry about the reac-
tion of the student body. What if everyone
sided with Billy? After all, he was the most
popular boy in the senior class. The big jock.
Abby could end up a virtual outcast at Central.

Frankie's next statement made her feel even
weirder. "So, Abby, I guess you won't be going
to the homecoming dance with Billy."

Lucy shot a mean glance at Frankie. "Shut
up, you dweeb. Don't say another word."

Frankie turned white. He had been on the
verge of asking Abby to the dance. After all,
she wasn't going steady with Billy anymore.
He had a right to try.

"I don't care about the homecoming dance,"
Abby replied. "I won't even go."

Frankie groaned. "Aw, Abby—"

Lucy scowled at him again. "Don't even think
it, geek-boy. She wouldn't go with you under
any circumstances."

Frankie tried to defend himself.

Lucy kept arguing with him.

But Abby didn't even hear them. Her eyes were focused on Central Academy in the distance. She had to face everyone, the whole student body.

She wondered if it was going to be horrible.

Probably.

FIVE

By lunchtime, Abby had to admit that the school day hadn't been too excruciating. She had been nervous, anticipating the first encounter with Billy. What would he say? What would he do? Would he be violent again?

In homeroom, there had been some whispers and sidelong glances. Everybody seemed to know. So far, however, her classmates had been understanding. The other cheerleaders had offered their condolences and a surprising number of people had said that they were glad she had broken off with Billy Major because he hadn't been right for her all along.

Abby had been pleased at the show of support from the girls. The boys took an entirely different slant. By noon, Abby had been asked on at least seven dates, six of them for the homecoming dance. She was free again, even though she hadn't given Billy back his ring yet. It was in the pocket of her jeans, heavy and cold.

Was it really over?

She had to see him sooner or later, even though they had no classes together.

As she strolled through the hall by herself, Abby mulled over the morning in her head.

First period had been English. The teacher showed part of the movie *The Grapes of Wrath* and reminded them that their term papers were due in a week. Abby was writing an essay about the romantic poets, her favorites.

Chemistry, her second period class, brought a surprise. She had forgotten all about the test. But when she bent over the exam paper, everything came back to her from the lecture. She finished the test, sure that she had aced it.

Third period was a dull lecture on world history, the Norman conquest of Britain. Abby tried to pay attention, but her concentration was shot. She ended up staring out the window, remembering the events of the previous day and night.

Right after history class, Abby realized that she'd forgotten to study for the vocabulary quiz in Latin. Luckily, she had study hall during fourth period, so she crammed for the test. She quizzed herself right before the bell rang, finding that she had committed everything to

memory. As she moved into the hallway, heading for the cafeteria, she figured she would go
over the lesson one last time during lunch.

A few students stared at her as she walked
along the corridor. But for the most part, no
one seemed too interested in Abby. Maybe the
excitement of the breakup had worn off. The
student body had moved on to other gossip.

"Abs, wait up!"

She heard Lucy behind her. Abby's tall,
dark-haired friend ran up beside her. "So,
how's it going on day one of The Breakup?"

Abby shrugged. "Not so bad."

"Really?"

"I haven't seen him yet," Abby said.

"Oh? Not once?"

Abby shook her head. "No, he's not in any
of my classes."

"How's everybody treating you?" Lucy asked
cautiously.

"Good. They all seem to be on my side."

"Hi, Abby!"

The voice had come from Frankie Deets. He
was gazing moon-eyed at Abby. She rolled her
eyes and just kept walking toward the cafeteria.

"You never should have given him a ride,"
Lucy teased. "Now he's going to be on your
case forever."

Abby grimaced, smiling wryly, assuming her

old posture of being superior to the geeks and
rabble. "Well, I do need a date for the homecoming dance!"

Lucy began to laugh. "You're such a mutant
magnet. A geek trap!"

They picked up the pace, leaving Frankie
behind. He was frowning with his hands in
his pockets. His narrow eyes watched as the
two girls exited the senior classroom building.

Abby and Lucy strode through the court-
yard. It was a beautiful fall day. Abby tensed
a little when she looked toward the football
stadium. It made her think of Billy.

"It's really over," she muttered to Lucy. "I
know it."

Lucy looked concerned. "Wow, I've never
seen you so serious. Are you okay?"

"Yes."

She felt the ring in her pocket. It was a burden, a cold weight that she needed to shed.
Maybe she would mail it to him.

"Let's eat," Lucy said. "I'm hungry."

They went through the serving line, choos-
ing light salads and Jell-O. As they moved
between the tables, voices buzzed and a few
more eyes glanced in Abby's direction. People
waved to her and Lucy. Abby overheard some
of the louder comments.

"She's really taking it well."

"Billy didn't break up with her, she broke off with *him*."

"I heard she kicked him in the—"

Abby nodded at a table in the middle of the cafeteria. "Let's sit there, Lucy. I want everyone to see how I'm doing."

"Perfect," Lucy replied. "Let them know that you're being strong."

They settled at the table, the center ring attraction. The news of the breakup had gained momentum by lunchtime. Abby was once again the hot topic of conversation.

Abby was laughing at a joke when she saw the fearful expression tighten Lucy's pretty face. Lucy gazed over Abby's shoulder. The noise level had risen in the cafeteria.

Abby turned to see Billy storming toward the table. His face was red. His eyes were wide. He was going to start trouble in front of the whole senior class.

"He's ballistic," Lucy whispered.

Abby quickly rose to her feet. "I have to get this over with. As soon as possible."

Billy stopped in his path when Abby turned to face him. He hadn't expected her to be so defiant. Though she was trembling inside, Abby steeled her expression and glared into his angry eyes.

"How are you feeling?" she asked mockingly. "A little sore?"

Billy took a few steps toward her, extending his hand. "I broke off with you. I want my ring back."

Abby cocked her head to regard the gawking students who were transfixed by the argument. "You hear that? Billy broke off with *me*. I'm free to date whoever I want."

A voice cheered from the back of the cafeteria, "All right!"

"I want my ring," Billy insisted.

"Maybe I don't have it," Abby replied. "Maybe I tossed it in the garbage."

"That was my senior class ring!"

Abby grimaced, suddenly bored by the whole thing. Billy was just a dweeb jock. She was too mature for him.

Billy pointed a finger at her. "You're gonna have to buy me another ring."

She thrust a hand into her jeans pocket. "Oh, here, take the stupid thing."

Withdrawing the hand, Abby opened her palm; the shiny surface reflected the dull glow of the overhead lights.

Billy reached for her palm. "Let me have it!"

Reflexively, Abby tossed the ring over Billy's shoulder. "Take it."

"You skank!" Billy cried.

He turned to see that his ring had landed in a trayful of mashed potatoes and meat loaf with gravy.

Everyone was laughing, pointing at Billy. He retrieved the ring from the tray and started back toward Abby. Abby cringed when she realized that Billy was raising his hand to strike her.

"No!" Lucy cried.

Billy came like a charging bull. Abby stood there, petrified, waiting for the inevitable blow—but it never hit her.

A dull thud resounded through the cafeteria. The spectators gasped as Billy's body shuddered and his legs buckled, his head snapping to one side.

Billy tumbled to the floor, grabbing his head. He squirmed, dropping the class ring. Abby lifted her eyes to see who had struck him.

Mrs. Seavey stood there with a lunch tray in her hand. She had whacked Billy with a pretty good shot to the temple. Abby could not believe that Mrs. Seavey had come to her rescue.

Mrs. Seavey waved a finger at Billy. "I don't care if you are a football star, mister. You don't treat one of my girls like that."

Billy glanced up with glassy eyes. "Gonna sue you!"

"Try it and I'll have you brought up on assault charges!"

A murmur went through the crowd that had circled to gawk at Billy. They were all talking about how Billy had started it. He was going to hit Abby. It was *his* fault, not Abby's!

Suddenly the ring of onlookers parted and a red-haired man stuck his face into the proceedings. "What's going on?"

Mrs. Seavey turned to regard the man. "Oh, Mr. Kinsley."

Harlan Kinsley served as the assistant principal of Central Academy. He was a stern man with a reputation for no-nonsense. Abby had never been in trouble before. Speechless, she just stood there, gaping at the man with accusing eyes.

Mrs. Seavey rose to Abby's defense. "There's no problem here," she said. "That boy just had a little fall. Didn't you?"

Mr. Kinsley's appearance had brought Billy into line. He didn't want to get in trouble either. He nodded in agreement.

"Break it up," Kinsley said.

As the crowd dispersed, Kinsley helped Billy to his feet. Mrs. Seavey had already tossed the lunch tray aside. Nobody spoke up in Billy's defense.

When the commotion had died down, Abby nodded at Mrs. Seavey. "Thanks. I mean—"

Mrs. Seavey smiled. "I won't have anyone treating a Central cheerleader like that."

Abby tried to smile back but the tears were flowing down her cheeks. Again she was at a loss for words. Her entire body was quaking.

Mrs. Seavey embraced her. "It's okay, Abby. There, there."

Abby cried on her shoulder, accepting comfort from the last person she expected to be sympathetic to her problems.

SIX

Mrs. Seavey studied the pyramid formed by the ten girls in practice sweats. "Steady! Abby, good form on the top. Everybody, hold your position like Abby!"

Abby stood at the summit of the triangular shape, rigid and motionless. She had never felt so poised, so confident. Mrs. Seavey had instilled her with a fresh sense of purpose. Abby knew Central could win in the spring cheer-offs.

"Perfect," Mrs. Seavey urged. "Hold it a minute longer."

Lucy grunted below on the second tier of the pyramid. "I can't last another minute."

"Shh!" Abby whispered.

Lucy rolled her eyes. Ever since the altercation in the cafeteria, Mrs. Seavey and Abby had been joined at the hip. Mrs. Seavey had drawn Abby into the spirit of the cheerleading squad competition. Of course, Lucy knew that Mrs. Seavey was the first adult to ever defend Abby. Abby's parents certainly weren't there when their daughter needed them.

Mrs. Seavey clapped her hands. "Okay, on three. Abby, dismount, the rest of you disengage!"

Abby focused on the practice field in the distance, keeping her concentration. Then, for a second, she saw Billy Major turn from the huddle to glare at her. It almost wrecked Abby's composure, but she managed to hold steady.

"One—"

Abby wasn't going to let the breakup affect her anymore.

"Two—"

It had been two days since the fight in the cafeteria and the big homecoming game was tomorrow.

"Three!"

Abby dived from the top of the pyramid, tucking into a ball. She rolled once on the ground, came up with a hand in the air and then dropped into a split. Behind her, the rest of the squad had disengaged from the pyramid. They executed one leg kick and froze behind Abby with their hands in the air.

Mrs. Seavey clapped her hands. "Perfect.

Abby you were just great. Everyone was perfect."

The girls cheered a little and giggled. Lucy knew that Abby's enthusiasm was catching. Still, Lucy was a little uneasy about Mrs. Seavey's friendship with Abby. Was Abby being manipulated for Mrs. Seavey's own selfish purposes?

"Now, I want to have a brief practice tomorrow before the game," Mrs. Seavey said.

"Aw, not then!"

"I have to do my hair!"

Lucy grimaced. "I thought we were ready."

Mrs. Seavey glanced at Abby.

Abby spoke up, defending the coach. "She's right. A warm-up wouldn't hurt. We can stretch."

"You just don't care because you don't have a date for the dance," one of the girls said angrily.

Mrs. Seavey glared at them. "That's enough."

Abby was blushing. She *didn't* have an escort for the homecoming dance. Several guys had asked her, but somehow she didn't feel ready to start dating again.

"We'll hold practice at four o'clock," Mrs. Seavey said. "For one hour. Then you'll have plenty of time to primp. The game doesn't start until six-thirty."

Abby suddenly felt guilty about betraying

the girls. They did need time to do their hair
and makeup before the game. They were all
lucky enough to have boyfriends.

Abby glanced at Mrs. Seavey, smiling. "Uh,
couldn't we stretch at six? That would give us
a half hour."

Mrs. Seavey sighed but then nodded. "Okay,
six o'clock. But we have to be ready to go by
kickoff."

Abby raised a fist in the air. "Central, number one!"

The girls rejoined in a rousing chorus, "Central, number one!"

"Six o'clock!" Mrs. Seavey repeated.

As they dispersed toward the locker room,
Lucy came over to Abby. "Thanks. The dragon-
queen would have us working twenty-four
hours a day if she—"

Abby's eyes narrowed. "Please, Lucy, don't
talk about Mrs. Seavey like that."

Lucy frowned. "When did you two become
best friends?"

"We're not!" Abby snapped. "She's just right
about certain things. If we're going to win that
cheer-off in the spring—"

"Abby!"

Mrs. Seavey approached them, putting her
arms around their shoulders. She gave Abby
and Lucy a hug. Lucy rolled her eyes and
looked away.

"My girls are the greatest," Mrs. Seavey said in a drippy tone. "We're going to look so *good* tomorrow night."

"Whatever you say, Mrs. Seavey," Lucy offered, tight-lipped.

Abby was a little embarrassed, but she smiled anyway. "We're going to work hard, Mrs. Seavey."

"I know you will."

Mrs. Seavey moved off, following the rest of the squad toward the locker room.

Lucy glared at Abby. "Is this for real? Or are you just being nice to her because of what she did to Billy?"

"I—I don't know, Lucy. It's just. . . . Nobody has ever tried to help me before. I've always been expected to be the best, the prettiest, the most popular. But Mrs. Seavey cares about me. She cares about all of us."

"Can't you see that she's using you?" Lucy pleaded. "She wants to get to us through you."

Abby's eyes flashed. "Oh yeah, it'd be a shame if we won that cheer-off in the spring. Or don't you want to be a winner?"

Lucy took a deep breath and sighed. "Okay, okay. Look, do you want to hang around with me and Jimmy at the dance?"

Abby's temper flared. "I don't need your pity, Lucy!"

"Abby, I wasn't—"

"Just drop dead!" Abby cried.

She ran off toward the locker room.

Lucy shook her head. What had gotten into Abby? It had been a rough week with the breakup and everything. Maybe Abby did have a right to be upset. Lucy wondered how she was going to apologize. Abby was her best friend. They had never fought before. They had to set things right.

As Lucy turned toward the locker room, she hesitated, glancing toward the football practice field. The field was empty. The team had already gone into the men's locker room.

As soon as Abby stormed away from Lucy, she regretted the spat. Lucy had only been trying to be nice. But Abby's pride had gotten the best of her. It hurt, not having a date for the homecoming dance—her last homecoming at Central.

She ran for the corridor that wound beneath the stadium to the girls' locker area. Autumn light diffused yellow and hazy over Port City. Abby moved into the cool shadows of the corridor.

Why had everything been so strange since the breakup? The world she had known before didn't seem to exist now. And why did she have a dreadful feeling that other bad things would happen to her? *Soon.*

Abby got all the way to the end of the corridor before she realized her mistake. The sign on the locker room door read BOYS. In her haste and anger she had taken the wrong hallway.

"Oh no," she muttered.

Abby turned away, hoping she could escape before anyone noticed that she had acted so foolishly. She ran through the shadows, making for the dull light at the end of the corridor. As she neared the red exit sign, she saw a towering shape fill the passageway, standing in silhouette against the glowing entrance.

"Hello, Abby."

She saw the number on the jersey, recognized the voice. Abby stopped dead in her tracks. There was no place to go, unless she went through Billy Major.

Abby's back pressed against the cold, concrete wall. "Don't come near me, Billy. I mean it."

He laughed a little. "Abby . . . I'm sorry about what happened, okay? I'm sorry about everything."

She tensed when he started to move toward her. "Billy, please—"

"No, you've got it all wrong. I don't want to hurt you, Abby. I still love you. I mean, weren't you coming in here to look for me?"

"No," Abby replied, "I just—"

Billy was almost on her now. "Listen, I'm sorry about everything." He stopped in front of her, blocking her escape.

"I'll scream, Billy. If you—"

He grimaced and shook his head. "No. It's not like that. I was out of line with the way I was treating you, Abby. I mean it. You were the best thing that ever happened to me. And I blew it."

Abby relaxed a little, trying to move sideways. "Well Billy, if that's how you feel, then let me go."

He stuck out his arm, trapping her against the wall for a moment. "Okay, I'll let you go. But you have to do something for me."

Abby closed her eyes, tensing again. "No, Billy."

He removed his arm, freeing her. But before she could flee, he took her hand, thrusting a cold, metallic object into her palm. Abby knew immediately that it was Billy's senior class ring.

"Billy, no, please—"

He squeezed her hand, closing it around the ring. "Just keep it until tomorrow night, Abby. If you want, you can give it back to me after the game. Okay?"

"Will you let me go?" Abby asked.

Billy stepped back, making room for her to

pass. "Hey, I never wanted to hurt you, Abs. And, I'll say it again. I'm sorry."

Abby hurried away from him. She gripped his class ring tightly in her hand. She intended to give it back again, right after the homecoming game.

But she would never get the chance.

SEVEN

The bright lights of the Central Academy Stadium bathed the gridiron in an eerie, yellow incandescence. Dover High had given Central a tough game, even though Central was supposed to win by a mile. Dover's defense had risen to the occasion, holding Billy Major to only thirty yards rushing.

Billy had scored Central's only touchdown in the first quarter. Central led 7–0 at the half. Dover scored on the first play from scrimmage at the beginning of the third quarter. Then, with less than one minute left in the game, Dover kicked a field goal to go ahead, 10–7.

Abby stood with the rest of the cheerleaders, circled at the ten yard line of Dover High. They anxiously awaited the kickoff. Suddenly, the homecoming game seemed like the most important thing in the world. And Central was going to lose to an inferior team.

Abby turned back to the squad. "All the way, Central!"

They dropped into formation, leading the booster section of the student body. Abby kept looking back at Lucy, who had ignored her since their fight after practice. Neither one of them had been humble enough to apologize, not yet anyway.

"All the way, Cen-tral! All the way!"

Abby glanced back over her shoulder to watch the kickoff. The ball went high into the air, arcing down to Billy on the twenty yard line of Central. He started to run straight ahead at full tilt.

Abby touched the ring that hung on a chain inside her sweater. She wasn't sure if she wanted to breakup anymore. Maybe she should give Billy a second chance.

Billy broke a long run on the kickoff return, taking the ball past the fifty yard line. After a time-out, the Central quarterback hit Billy with a screen pass. Billy broke another big run and then stepped out of bounds right in front of Abby.

He stopped and smiled at her. "I'm gonna win this game for you, Princess!"

Abby smiled back.

Billy darted onto the field.

Abby bounced on her feet and raised her

arm in the air. "Punch the line, Central!"

As the football team huddled, the squad went into a cheer. Only twenty seconds remained on the clock. And Central had no more time-outs. They had to score on this play or the game was lost.

The home crowd went wild as Billy took the ball. He hit the line, but he had no room to run. He was going to be tackled for a loss.

No! Billy turned to the outside, rounding the end in a burst of speed. He shot past the Dover linebackers and then took a defensive back with him into the end zone. The gun sounded to end the game. Central 13, Dover 10.

The cheerleading squad danced like mad girls. They were hugging each other, and yelling, acting like grade schoolers. Abby suddenly found herself embracing Lucy.

Lucy had tears in her eyes. "I'm sorry!"

"No, I'm sorry more!"

Lucy wiped her eyes. "Billy has been calling everyone saying he wants you back."

"I know. I have his ring," Abby replied.

"What are you gonna do?" Lucy asked.

But Abby was suddenly whisked away in a wave of human tide as the spectators ran onto the field. She turned to see Billy being hoisted into the air by his teammates. They carried him toward the entrance of the locker room.

Abby and the rest of the cheerleading squad

fell in beside the team, rooting them on. Abby suddenly felt elated, glad to be part of the victory. She looked up to find Billy's face focused on her. He nodded and grinned.

Abby didn't know what to do. Billy had once been nice to her. Could he change back to the old Billy?

The team disappeared down the corridor, taking Billy Major with them.

Abby found Lucy again, hugging her. "We won."

Lucy looked her in the eye. "Did *you* win?"

"I don't know," Abby replied.

"Are you going to take him back?" Lucy asked.

Abby shrugged. If she did take Billy back, it would have to be a slow process. She'd have to know that he was sincere.

The other cheerleaders circled around Abby and Lucy. They had to get ready for the homecoming dance in the gym. Abby frowned a little because she didn't have a date. But then, someone said that Billy Major didn't have a date either.

Lucy glanced at Abby again. "I have to go. Jimmy is waiting for me at the gym."

Abby said, "I think I'll wait for Billy."

Lucy winked. "I hope it all turns out for the best."

"I hope so too," Abby replied.

Abby leaned back against the concrete wall, wondering if Billy wanted to take her to the dance. Abby had brought a nice dress, leaving it in the minivan. She had planned to go by herself but now she might have a date after all.

"Oh, Billy," she muttered.

He had been so great to her in the beginning. Maybe his selfish behavior was just temporary. Abby decided she would gladly take back the old Billy, the one who had given her his ring.

She touched her bosom again, to feel the weight of the gold ring. "Oh no!"

The ring wasn't there! It was gone. Abby found the broken chain inside her sweater. The ring must have snapped off and dropped somewhere between the field and the locker room.

She had to find the ring. Even if she was breaking up with Billy—which now seemed tentative at best—he still had a right to get his ring back. Abby had to search for it.

Absently, she started to retrace her steps, gazing at the ground. The ring could have broken loose anywhere during the commotion after the game. It had to be somewhere on the ground. Unless someone had already found it.

"Please," Abby said to herself. "Let *me* find it."

But the night was too dark for her to see in every shadow. As she turned toward the field, the lights went off in the stadium, leaving it totally black. Abby wasn't ready to give up, though. She had a flashlight in the glove compartment of the van. If it took all night, she was going to find that ring.

Hurrying to the parking lot, Abby moved between the cars toward the van. She opened the door of the van and retrieved the flashlight. As she was closing the door, she thought she heard someone moving behind her.

"Who's there?" she asked the shadows.

But there was no reply. Abby heard some more shuffling of feet on the ground. She shined the beam of the flashlight but saw nothing except empty cars.

Using the flashlight to illuminate the way, she returned to the football field. Where had she been standing? At the end zone. She had felt the ring earlier. Had it come loose while they were all jumping around after the winning score?

Abby aimed the beam at the ground, searching along the white stripe of the field markings.

"It has to be here," she whispered to herself.

Something thumped behind her. Abby hesitated, flashing the beam in the direction of the noise. A stiff breeze swept suddenly over the field, rattling some of the debris that had been left behind in the stadium.

Abby just wanted to find the ring and get back to the locker room. Good or bad, she had to deal with Billy. She still wasn't sure that she would take him back.

Again she scanned the ground, hoping to see the ring. If someone else found it, at least they would see Billy's name engraved inside it. Maybe they would return it.

She had begun to grow more impatient. What if Billy had already come out of the locker room? Would he be expecting her to attend the dance on his arm? What could one dance hurt, even if they decided to call it quits? And he *had* made the effort to apologize.

Scuffling footsteps rose on the breeze. Abby's head snapped up. She swung the flashlight, but there didn't seem to be anyone there. The wind was playing tricks on her.

The ring!

She had to keep looking. She followed the sideline marker of the field; the ring had to be here somewhere. She couldn't tell Billy, the football hero, that she had lost his prized possession.

Another noise behind her.

Abby didn't look this time. She figured it was only a paper cup rattling against the bleachers in the stiff breeze. Her eyes were fixed to the ground in hopes of seeing the ring.

"Come on! Please let me find it."

The beam of light touched something that glinted back at Abby. Her heart stopped. Had she really found it?

She searched for a moment but the golden gleaming seemed to be gone. Sweat poured from her brow even in the breeze of the autumn night. It had to be there.

Again, the sharp glint of something shiny appeared in the narrow wake of the beam.

Abby stepped toward the glittering object, holding her breath. It had to be. It just had to be the ring!

Her hand reached down, gripping the object. The gold was chilly against her skin. She had the ring. Billy wouldn't be disappointed now.

"Abby!"

She heard her name through the wind.

"Who's there?" she called.

The beam of the flashlight swung over the empty benches where the home team had been sitting.

Had she really heard someone call her name?

Or was it just another trick of the wind?

Abby felt a chilly breeze on her neck. A shiver ran up her spine. Now that she had the ring tightly in her grasp, it was best just to head back to the gymnasium. She wouldn't even stop at the van to get her dress.

She took a few steps forward.

"Abby!"

She stopped, lifting the beam. "Who's there?"

Nothing.

Were those the sounds of feet shuffling in the night? She turned a half-circle, searching for movement.

"This isn't funny," she said to the wind.

No reply.

Abby started to walk again. When her feet hit the oval track around the field, she thought she heard footsteps behind her. She wheeled with the beam, catching a brief glimpse of someone ducking into the stairwell of the stadium bleachers.

"Who's there?" she called.

It couldn't be Billy. Or could it? Maybe he had showered and come looking for her. But he had no way of knowing that she had returned to the field to look for his ring.

"Billy?"

The only reply was the muffled rush of wind that swirled around her shoulders, chilling her.

Abby turned away from the stadium again, hurrying on the oval track. She didn't have far to go. As soon as she reached the gymnasium, everything would be all right. Besides, she thought, what was there to worry about except the wind and the shadows playing tricks on her?

But the wind and the shadows could never produce the sound of running footsteps behind her. Abby turned and shined the flashlight on the form that rushed forward in the darkness. Someone—something—was almost upon her.

Abby started to run, but slipped on an empty bag of popcorn left over from the game. She stumbled a few steps which allowed the intruder to catch her. The hurtling weight of the attacker knocked Abby to the ground.

Abby screamed. No one heard her cries above the wind. The attacker grabbed her hair, yanking hard.

"No!" Abby pleaded. "Don't."

The monster bent down, breathing hot breath on Abby's face. "You're mine!" said a gravelly voice.

Abby began to struggle, trying to get out from under the weight of her attacker. She didn't recognize the voice and couldn't see the face.

"Help me!" she wailed.

A balled fist struck the back of her head. Abby felt stunned for a moment. The intruder's dead weight pinned her to the surface of the track.

"What do you want from me?" Abby pleaded.

"You're mine," the raspy voice repeated.

The intruder's weight shifted a little. Abby realized she was still gripping the flashlight. When her attacker shifted, momentarily freeing her, Abby flipped over and swung the flashlight with all her strength, catching the monster in the elbow.

Abby heard a loud crack. The attacker rolled off her, groaning. Abby started to scurry to her feet. She had to get away, to make it to the safety of the gymnasium where her friends could help her.

She was up and about to run when the hand closed around her ankle. Abby tripped again, falling toward the track. She managed to break the fall with her hands, her palms scraping against the asphalt surface.

The intruder shuffled behind her.

Abby crawled forward, trying to get up again.

"No," she sobbed, "please don't—"

She staggered to her feet, stumbling toward the gym in the darkness. Her head spun from the blow delivered by the attacker. Abby wanted to run but her legs would not cooperate.

"You're mine!"

The footsteps drew closer as the attacker

rushed again from the shadows.

Abby lifted the flashlight to strike. The monster grabbed her hand, stopping her. For a moment, Abby was face to face with her assailant. She saw that her attacker was wearing a black ski mask. It could have been anyone hiding behind it.

"No!" Abby cried. "Someone help me!"

The attacker's fist smashed into Abby's forehead. Abby reeled backward, losing her balance as her legs went dead. The intruder hit her again. Abby went down.

"You're mine!"

Abby tried to raise herself up again. But the blow to the back of her head had done it's damage. Abby closed her eyes and drifted into unconsciousness.

EIGHT

Abby sensed movement all around her. She could not see yet, but she didn't care about that. Her entire being had been overcome with an incredible lightness, a buoyant, joyous feeling of rapture. She had no immediate recollection of what had happened to her. The horror of the football field had faded, replaced by the ethereal bliss that had seized her.

Sounds faded in, voices from nowhere.

"Is she all right?"

Mom!

"What are you doing for her?"

Dad!

Her parents were there, both of them! They stood by her side. She wanted to embrace them, to tell them how much she loved them. But she found that she couldn't speak.

"Doctor," her mother said, "what happened?"

An unfamiliar voice filtered through the haze. "She was attacked. Bludgeoned with a blunt instrument of some sort."

Bludgeoned? Attacked? Abby couldn't remember anything like that. She only knew that she felt great, elated, rapturous.

Her father sounded like he was ready to cry. "My God, have the police . . . ?"

"Yes," the doctor replied.

Her mother was crying. "Will she—I mean . . ."

The doctor sighed. "I think she'll be all right. There may be some brain damage—"

Her father's voice rose quickly. "Brain damage? My God, what was she hit with?"

"We're not sure," the doctor replied. "The forensic investigators will know more when they review the evidence. My guess is that it was some kind of club."

Hey, I'm all right, Abby thought. Don't cry, Mom. Dad, I'm okay. None of that stuff happened.

Mrs. Wilder spoke in a whisper. "Doctor, was she . . . I mean . . . did the attacker . . . ?"

"Molest her?" the doctor said, finishing the sentence. "We don't think so. At least—"

Mr. Henry Wilder was on the verge of going into a rage. "You don't *think* so? What kind of place are you running here?"

"Relax," the doctor said. "She wasn't raped, to be specific."

"Thank God," her mother replied. "Thank God."

What are they talking about? Abby wondered. Nothing happened to me. I would remember it.

"What *did* happen to her?" Mr. Wilder asked anxiously.

The doctor sighed. "When they found your daughter, she wasn't wearing any clothes."

"I'll kill whoever did this!" Mr. Wilder cried. "I swear I'll murder the son of a—"

"Take it easy," the doctor said softly. "Something happened, but we think that her attacker was scared off before he could do anything more to hurt her."

Mrs. Wilder sighed. "We never should have let her go to that game by herself."

"Who scared him off?" Mr. Wilder asked.

"You'll have to ask the police," the doctor replied. "Though I heard it was a member of the stadium maintenance crew."

"I'll kill whoever did this!" Mr. Wilder repeated.

I'm okay, Abby thought. Hey, Mom and Dad, don't worry. I feel fine.

But there was more movement around Abby. She heard the police chief talking to her parents. They were still looking for the man who had attacked Abby.

"What about that kid?" Mr. Wilder asked. "The one that Abby was dating?"

"He's a suspect," the official voice replied. "They're all suspects until we can get a better picture of what happened."

Mrs. Wilder began to bawl. "It's our fault, Henry. We were never with her. She wanted to talk to me the other day, but I was too busy."

"I'll find whoever did this and kill him," Mr. Wilder muttered.

The police chief shook his head. "No you won't. We're going to find out who did this to your daughter."

Did what? Abby wondered. I'm fine. Can't you all see me? I feel great!

"Any idea what she was doing on the field so late?" the police chief asked. "It was dark."

Neither one of her parents had a clue.

Abby suddenly remembered the ring. She had gone back to find Billy's lost ring. And she *had* found it!

"We'll keep in touch," the police chief said. "If she should come out of the coma—"

Coma?

But I'm fine, Abby thought. I—

She had a sudden sensation of floating. Her body seemed to rise, though it wasn't her body at all. Lights came into focus as she gazed down on a scene below her.

A girl lay in a hospital bed with tubes and needles sticking out of her. The girl's head had been bandaged. She had bruises all over her face and arms.

A doctor stood beside the bed gazing at the girl. Two adults stood on the other side of the bed, crying. It was a pitiful scene. Then Abby realized that she was looking at herself and her own parents.

"It's me," she said to no one.

How could she be floating over her own bed? Was she dead? No, they all seemed to think the girl in the bed was alive. It couldn't be Abby. She felt wonderful.

"Abby?"

"Yes?" she replied to the scene below her.

"No, Abby, turn away from there. Come to us, Abby."

Abby experienced a feeling of turning around, like a spaceship in zero gravity. She saw a bright light in front of her eyes. It was almost blinding, though she felt serene when she gazed into the eerie glow.

Someone or something moved toward her. Abby sensed the presence of two girls. Only they weren't really girls. They looked like angels, floating in a sea of nothingness.

Abby had only one question for the unearthly creatures. "Am I dead?"

But the spirits did not answer right away.

The lights of the hospital waiting area were stark and cold in Lucy's eyes. She could not believe what had happened to her best friend. Why had Abby been all alone on the football field, wandering around in the darkness?

Lucy sighed and lifted her gaze to the nurse's station. When would she get to see Abby? So far the only people allowed in the intensive care unit were the doctors and Abby's parents. Lucy figured she probably wouldn't get to see Abby, at least not today. But she was going to stay in hopes of a momentary visit, a chance to talk to her.

"Let me through!"

Lucy heard the all-too-familiar voice echoing through the sterile-smelling hallways. Mrs. Seavey barreled toward the nurse's station with a frenzied expression on her chubby face. Lucy grimaced for a moment, but then she softened, realizing that Mrs. Seavey really *did* care about Abby and the other cheerleaders.

Mrs. Seavey rushed past Lucy, attacking the nurse's station with her massive presence. "I want to know how Abby Wilder is doing!" she demanded. "Now!"

The duty nurse wore a tight-lipped scowl.

"We are not allowed to release that information at this time."

Mrs. Seavey argued, but to no avail. She turned away from the station, wiping her sweaty forehead, and staggered toward the waiting area with a dazed look in her eyes.

Then she saw Lucy waiting there. "Oh my God, Lucy! How can it be? How can it be?"

Lucy felt compelled to stand up, to greet Mrs. Seavey with open arms. They both cried together, embracing, comforting each other. Some of Lucy's animosity toward Mrs. Seavey began to fade. Maybe Abby had been right about their coach.

Lucy drew away. Mrs. Seavey reached into a pocket for a tissue to wipe the tears from her round cheeks. She had an extra one for Lucy.

"What happened?" she asked Lucy. "I heard that she was hit in the head."

Lucy nodded. "That's all I heard. Frankie Deets said he got a look at the ambulance as they were putting her in—" She choked on emotion for a moment. "—Frankie said her head had been bandaged."

Mrs. Seavey threw out her hands. "Where did she go? What did she do?"

Lucy leaned closer, whispering. "She was waiting for Billy."

Mrs. Seavey's face grew red, angry, wide-eyed. "I should have known! That kid is nothing but trouble. I don't see why Abby ever went out with him."

"He wasn't always mean to her," Lucy replied, feeling a weird urge to defend Billy all of a sudden.

Mrs. Seavey swayed for a second, wobbling on her stubby legs. She stumbled toward a plastic chair, falling with a dull plopping sound. Lucy sat next to her, waiting again.

"Will they let us in to see her?" Mrs. Seavey asked.

Lucy shrugged. "They haven't let me in, not so far."

Mrs. Seavey drew a shuddering breath. "If only she hadn't gone with him!"

Lucy frowned. "She went with Billy? I mean, do you know for sure that it—"

"Who else could it be?" Mrs. Seavey argued. "He was all over her in the cafeteria."

Lucy shook her head. "I don't know."

"Abby told me that he tried to attack her at her house," Mrs. Seavey said. "Is that true?"

"Yes," Lucy replied.

Mrs. Seavey scowled at the walls. "I knew it."

Lucy sighed and stared at the floor. "I guess it could be Billy. I just never thought he was capable of something like that."

Mrs. Seavey waved a finger in the air. "Oh, you just listen up, young lady. Males always

have it in them to hurt us. Even the late Mr.
Seavey showed me the back of his hand more
than once. But I never took it lying down, I
can tell you!"

"Mrs. Seavey?"

"Yes, dear?"

Lucy suddenly flashed back to the locker
room, just as she had been leaving to go to
the gym. "You were looking for Abby after the
game, weren't you?"

"Yes, I was," Mrs. Seavey replied. "I was
going to congratulate her for a job well done.
Oh, if only I had reached her before—"

Lucy began to cry. "You might have saved
her. Why did she go down to the football field
in the dark?"

"Maybe he dragged her," Mrs. Seavey offered. "Maybe—"

Lucy's head jerked toward the corridor as
a loud commotion resounded in the hallway.
Lucy recognized the bellowing voice immediately.

"Billy!" she whispered.

Mrs. Seavey stood up, glaring in the direction of Billy Major. "How can he come here
after—my God!"

Billy barreled through the hallway, with
Frankie Deets close behind. Billy slammed
into an orderly who carried a metal tray,
which clanged against the wall and crashed

to the floor. He charged up to the nurse's station and demanded to see his girlfriend.

"Am I dead?"

Abby asked the question again after the spirits—if that was what they were—did not answer. There were definitely two of them. Abby perceived one to be larger than the other. They could have been girls, but it was difficult to tell in the hazy glow.

Abby tried to focus on their faces, though she was aware that they had no physical presence in this place. It was like shadows or ripples in a current. Things shifted, whirlpooling in gentle eddies of light. The faces of her hosts had no real shape, but created a warm sensation that filled Abby with a glow of well-being.

Still, she was curious. "Okay, if you won't tell me if I'm dead or not—"

"You're not dead," said the little spirit in a voice that sounded like music.

"Silence!" the larger and, as it seemed, elder spirit said in a strident tone.

Yet, it was still music—music and light were all that seemed to exist here.

Abby tried to look beyond the gentle spirits, but she could see only the bright light. "Where is this place?"

The elder spirit pulsed with a low humming

vibration. "You cannot understand."

"Try me," Abby replied. "I was pretty good in school at Central. I—I mean—"

She turned back suddenly, gazing toward the place she had left behind. All she could see now was the hospital bed and her own body. The window to the other world had gotten smaller.

"I can't go back, can I?" she asked in a little voice.

The smaller one gave a musical laugh. "Can't you?"

"But where am I?"

The elder sprite spoke in a riddle. "You are on the other side, in the realm of neverending possibilities."

"I don't understand," Abby said.

The elder spirit buzzed and crackled for a second, like a bug lamp zapping a fly.

Abby kept staring at herself in the hospital bed. Her body seemed to be on the verge of death. Yet, her spirit—it had to be her spirit—flourished in this exceptional light.

The elder spirit dimmed a little. "I must leave."

Abby turned back to her hosts. "But you haven't—"

Before she could utter another word, the spirit vanished into nothingness. Abby was left alone with the smaller bundle of light. Suddenly, a girl's face appeared clear and bright on the flickering creature. The face was smiling.

Abby thought she was also smiling—if she had a face herself. "Hi," she said. "Who are you?"

"I have no name."

"What is this place?" Abby asked. "Where am I? What do I do now?"

"I'm not supposed to say. There's a rule against telling. There are many rules on this side," the spirit replied. "Just like your world."

"Rules?"

"Yes, Abby."

"What kind of rules?"

The ethereal girl giggled a little. "Rules than can be broken. And if you let me, I'll show you how to break a few of them!"

Abby basked in the warmth of the light. "Is it always like this here? Huh?"

But the other spirit was fading now.

"See you later, Abby. Don't worry."

Abby felt a sudden pang of loneliness. Sighing, she looked back down at the bed. The window was growing wide again. And Abby could hear someone calling her name.

NINE

"Abby? Abby, please wake up! Abby, can you hear me? Oh no, Abby, please—"

Mrs. Wilder wept over the battered body of her daughter. Abby's physical presence lay in the hospital bed with tubes and needles stuck in her. Mrs. Wilder stroked the white skin of Abby's delicate cheekbone.

Mr. Wilder bent down, touching his wife's shoulder. "Honey, I think we should leave now."

"I want to stay," Mrs. Wilder sobbed. "I want to be here when my little girl wakes up."

Police Chief Victor Danridge also stood beside the hospital bed. He was a tall, sandy-haired, green-eyed man in a gray suit. He was also Port City's chief investigator of violent crime, like attempted murder.

"Mrs. Wilder," Danridge said softly, "we

have to let the doctors and nurses take care of her. She's incapable—what on earth is going on out there?"

Someone was causing trouble. A boy's shrill voice rose outside the intensive care unit, demanding to see Abby, calling her his girlfriend.

Mr. Wilder's face grew red. "It's that punk, Billy Major! He's the one who did this!"

"Wait a minute," Danridge cried, reaching for Mr. Wilder.

But Henry Wilder was too quick for the police chief. He darted from the intensive care unit, rushing toward the sound of Billy Major's shouting. Billy turned and saw Abby's father coming at him.

"Uh, Mr. Wilder—"

Henry Wilder pointed a finger at Billy. "You little creep. You hurt my daughter."

Mr. Wilder lunged for Billy, catching him by the throat. Billy tried to fight, but Mr. Wilder was too strong. He pushed Billy against the wall and started to choke him.

"Wilder! Stop that!" Chief Danridge cried.

"He's going to pay!" cried Abby's father.

Across the hall in the waiting room, Mrs. Seavey, Lucy, and Frankie watched in amazement. Billy's face started turning dark red. But then the police chief was on Henry Wilder, dragging him away from the stunned boy.

"I wish I could do the same to that kid," Mrs.

Seavey muttered. "He deserves it."

Lucy grimaced, a little shocked by the histrionics. "We don't even know if he did it, Mrs. Seavey."

The chubby woman nodded her head. "Oh, he did it, all right. You can take that to the bank."

Chief Danridge nodded to one of the hospital security guards, who had run into the waiting area from the hallway. "You, get a doctor to look at this kid."

Billy came off the wall. "I don't have to take this! I'm outta here!"

Danridge pushed Henry Wilder to one side. The police chief reached into his coat, pulling out a thirty-eight caliber police revolver. Billy gaped at the weapon, standing dead in his tracks.

"Nobody's leaving this room," Danridge said.

Lucy found herself gasping.

Mrs. Seavey did the same.

Frankie's eyes bulged and he swallowed hard. Henry Wilder and his wife were also transfixed by the sight of the pistol.

"As soon as everybody has calmed down," Danridge said, keeping the weapon on Billy, "we're all going to sit down and have a nice little chat."

No one, especially Billy Major, chose to disagree.

• • •

Abby thought she was shaking her head, even though she wasn't sure she even had one in this new realm. "They're all making such a fuss over me."

The flickering ball of light had returned and seemed to giggle. "Yes, they are making a fuss. They must really love you."

Abby wanted to know more about this entity that came and went as it pleased. "You said there were rules on this side."

"Rules exist throughout the universe, except in the darkness. There lies chaos. But you don't have to worry."

"Have you ever been to the other side, to—earth, is it? I—I'm not sure what to call it anymore," Abby said.

"I wouldn't remember if I had been," the spirit replied. "There's no memory here. That's one of the rules."

Abby looked back at the square opening that reminded her of a television screen. "But I have *my* memory. I know I was there. I—I was a senior at Central. Someone hurt me. But who? I don't remember."

"You might remember before you go."

"But why can *I* remember the other side?" Abby asked.

The spirit giggled again. "That's how I know you *are* going back. Because you remember.

Those who are going back always remember."

Abby wasn't sure she was relieved about going back. She didn't feel much of anything except the divine sensation of well-being. It was happiness, a thousandfold.

"How long will I be here?" Abby asked.

"It's not important. There's no time here, not the way you perceive time. It's always forever. That's another rule of this realm."

"This could all be happening in my mind," Abby offered philosophically. "All in my mind."

"It could be," the tender spirit replied. "Now, I want you to tell me what it's like on the other side. I always talk to the ones who remember, but I never get tired of hearing about it."

"Will you tell me about this side?" Abby asked.

"I can't."

"The rules?" Abby asked.

"Yes. We don't want the ones on the other side to know too much about this side."

"But *I* know," Abby said. "I see this, the light, and those whirling shapes, like clouds."

"No. You only see what you have been permitted to see. This is a door. Not the realm. You will be going back soon. You—"

Something crackled and the elder spirit appeared out of nowhere. Just then, Abby felt another dark jolt. The other world was calling her again.

Billy Major shifted nervously in a plastic chair in the hospital waiting room. "This is bogus," he said. "You've been talking to us for over an hour. I want to go home, Chief. Hey, you hear me?"

Chief Danridge focused his accusing green eyes on the hostile boy. "Billy, that's enough. I'll let you go when I've gotten the information that I need."

"Why don't you just arrest me?" Billy challenged.

Danridge sighed. "Nobody's going to be arrested, at least not tonight. Now, give me a minute to look over my notes."

Danridge had scribbled on a small pad during his interrogation of almost everyone in the waiting room—Billy, Lucy, Mrs. Seavey, Mr. and Mrs. Wilder. He had asked them questions over and over, trying to piece together what had happened to Abby. So far, there weren't any concrete answers, or even the hint of a solution.

Lucy glanced over at Mrs. Wilder, who was still crying. Mr. Wilder sat next to his wife, his arm wrapped around her shoulder. Abby's father glared at Billy. Mrs. Seavey was also casting daggers at the arrogant youth.

Danridge looked up from his notes. "Billy, you say you dressed after the game and then went straight to the dance?"

Billy nodded. "Yeah, that's right."

"Did anyone walk with you from the locker room to the gymnasium?" Danridge asked.

"I did!" Frankie Deets piped up for the first time. He had been sitting in the corner, all but forgotten. He seemed eager to defend Billy.

Danridge hadn't questioned Frankie yet. "You left the locker room with Billy?"

"Yeah," Frankie replied. "He was looking for Abby."

Billy grimaced. "Thanks, Deets!"

"Look," Frankie rejoined, "we went straight to the dance. Billy never saw Abby. That's why we came here when we heard that she had been hurt."

Danridge stared at Frankie, not saying a word. Sometimes the quiet ones could cause a lot of trouble, the police chief thought. Frankie Deets looked nervous. Was he hiding something?

Danridge turned back to Billy. "You got rough with the girl. That's what Lucy said."

Lucy shifted in her seat, looking away from Billy.

Billy slumped in the chair, frowning and shaking his head. "I didn't mean to. It just—I told her I was sorry, okay. I gave her my ring again. She was gonna tell me tonight if we could get back together."

Mr. Wilder leaned forward. "You attacked her! Admit it, you little bag of puke!"

Mrs. Seavey pointed a finger at Billy. "He's violent. He should be locked up!"

Billy glared back at her. "Violent, huh! You were the one who slammed me in the head with a lunch tray, you fat—"

Danridge snapped, "That's enough!"

There was some grumbling, but everyone obeyed the order.

Danridge cast his searching gaze on Mrs. Seavey. "You hit Billy here with a lunch tray?"

Mrs. Seavey blushed. "All right, I'll admit it. But he was going to hurt Abby. He was running toward her with his fist in the air."

"Was not!" Billy lied, trying to defend himself.

"You were going to hit her," Mrs. Seavey insisted. "Ask anyone who was there. The whole cafeteria saw it. Lucy saw it!"

Lucy blushed at the sound of her name.

Danridge glanced at the dark-haired girl. "Is this true, Lucy? Billy was going to attack Abby in the cafeteria?"

Reflexively, Lucy's eyes flickered toward Billy, whose face was reddening in anger. "I do think he was going to hit her," Lucy said.

Billy threw out his hands, leaning toward Danridge. "I got a little bit out of line! That's it."

Mr. Wilder bared his teeth. "I oughta—"

Abby's mother sobbed with her face in her hands. "Why did you do it, Billy? Why?"

Billy came out of the chair and dropped to his knees before her. "I swear, Mrs. Wilder, I never did anything to hurt Abby. Maybe I came on a little too strong, but I wouldn't do something like this. I *couldn't* do this to Abby. I love her!"

"Save it for the jury," Mr. Wilder replied sarcastically.

Danridge told Billy to go back to his seat. Billy sank into the chair. He winced suddenly and grabbed his elbow.

"What's wrong?" Danridge asked.

Billy shrugged. "Just a strawberry from the game."

"Let me see," Danridge said. "Take off your jacket."

Billy reluctantly took off his sports coat. He had a bruise and an abrasion on his elbow. Danridge studied the wound, thinking of the flashlight they had found a few feet away from Abby's body. The glass lens of the light had been broken, obviously used as a weapon by Abby because there had been no shards of glass in her wounds. Could the flashlight have caused the marks on Billy's elbow?

"We'll need a blood sample from Billy," Danridge said to the security guard. "Tell the hospital to get his parents on the line. We'll need them to sign some papers before we can take blood."

Billy's eyes narrowed. "Blood sample? For what?"

"Evidence," Danridge replied. "We'll tell your parents all about it. Besides, if you're innocent, the tests will prove you didn't hurt Abby."

"I didn't!"

Danridge looked around the semicircle of suspects. "Abby went to that dark field by herself. We think she could have been lured away. Or, went back for some other reason. Something she'd forgotten, perhaps.

Mrs. Seavey stiffened. "It wasn't because we had left any of our cheerleading gear behind. We clear the field after every game."

Frankie Deets spoke up again. "Maybe she lost something."

"Does anyone have any idea," Danridge asked, "what she might have lost?"

Lucy leaned forward. "Wait a minute. The ring. She was wearing Billy's ring around her neck. Maybe it came loose."

Danridge sighed and looked at his notes. They hadn't found any high school class ring at the site of the attack. There *had* been a small piece of gold chain, however.

"We have to search you, Billy. The Deets kid, too."

"What!" Billy cried.

Frankie Deets had turned an ashen color. "Search me?"

Danridge conducted the frisking himself. He was hoping to come up with a class ring, but he wasn't so lucky. Neither of the boys could really be linked to the crime scene, not yet anyway.

When they were back in their seats, Danridge looked at the cheerleading coach. "You can go, Mrs. Seavey."

"Oh. Well, thank you, Mr. Danridge. If I can be of any help to you—"

"I'll call you," Danridge replied. "Deets, hit the bricks. And make sure you have your parents call me."

Frankie was up like a flash. "Yes, sir." He fled the sterile smell of the hallways, passing Mrs. Seavey on his way to the elevator.

"Can I go?" Billy asked.

"Sit tight," Danridge replied. "Mr. and Mrs. Wilder, you should go home, get some rest."

Mr. Wilder nodded. "Don't let this punk out of your sight. Because if you do. . . ."

Danridge glared at Abby's father. "Don't make threats that will come back to haunt you," the chief warned.

Mr. Wilder led his wife away from the intensive care unit. When they caught up to Mrs. Seavey, Abby's mother thanked the chubby woman for being so supportive. Mrs. Seavey began to cry along with Abby's mother.

Lucy still sat on the edge of her chair. "What about me?"

Danridge nodded toward the elevator. "You can go. Unless there's something else you can think of that might help me?"

Lucy shook her head. "No . . . just—I don't think Billy did this to Abby."

"Why do you think that?" Danridge asked.

Lucy shrugged. "I just do."

"Thanks," Billy said to her softly.

Lucy got up, leaving the waiting area. But she did not go straight to the elevator. Instead, she slipped past the nurse's station and went straight into Abby's room.

Lucy stood by the bed, gazing down at her best friend. She took Abby's hand. It felt so small and lifeless.

"Come back to us, Abs. Please."

Lucy had no idea that Abby Wilder could hear her every word.

TEN

"I'm coming back, Lucy!" Abby cried. "Don't worry."

The elder spirit hovered nearby. "She can't hear you, Abby. But you're right. You must go back."

The little spirit gave what amounted to an ethereal sigh. "Yes, you must leave us."

Abby turned to the spirits. She didn't feel sadness, but the bliss of her ghostly state had dimmed. There seemed to be a heaviness that she perceived, like the drawing current of a whirlpool tide.

"You can sense it," the elder spirit said.

"Yes," Abby replied. "I'm going back. I know it."

Her own spirit shape had begun to ebb, growing dimmer with each passing second. Abby could sense time again as she was fording the narrow barrier between the two worlds.

"Will I remember this?" Abby asked the elder spirit.

"We cannot say."

"Can you help me?"

"No," the spirit replied. "We are not allowed to interfere."

The material world tugged her toward the window.

"I want to know," Abby said. "Tell me who did this to me?"

"I cannot," the elder spirit replied sadly.

But as she was fading from the light, the smaller entity dashed forward, virtually crashing through Abby's very soul. Abby felt the little spirit's presence for a moment. And she knew! The little spirit told her who had done this heinous deed to Abby, something she could never have conceived in the earthly plane.

Abby experienced the sensation of soaring downward, a parachutist in the air currents. She slipped back into the realm of the senses, rejoining her body. Abby's eyes flickered open. She saw Lucy standing there, holding her hand.

Lucy cried out, calling for the nurse. "She's awake!"

Abby knew she was in her body again. The pain penetrated her every cell. For a moment, she remembered the two spirits and the world of light. But then the agony of her body became too great, forcing her eyes shut and erasing the memory of the other side.

Abby slept now without dreams.

The next Monday at Central, everyone was talking about Abby's miraculous awakening. Billy Major, who had subsequently been released by the police, was spreading the word as fast as his lips could flap. By the time the rumor mill churned it back to Lucy herself, the story had her healing Abby with a laying on of hands. Lucy wasn't quite sure that she'd done a miracle or anything; she was just glad that Abby was back among the living.

Lucy walked down the hallway of the senior classroom building, heading for her locker. Everyone smiled or nodded to her. Lucy had always been part of the popular crowd, but now she was even more special. She had been there when Abby came back from the dead.

The school day had been like a waking dream for Lucy. She hadn't been able to sleep all night. Even though Abby had opened her eyes, she still wasn't out of the darkness just yet. The attack had left her bruised, dazed, and in pain. It might be a long road to recovery, especially with her head wounds.

As Lucy approached her locker, she saw Billy Major standing there, leaning against the wall of lockers. His face was taut, his eyes fixed on nothing. Lucy started to back away, to avoid him, but Billy turned suddenly to see her.

He smiled. "Hey, Lucy. I—I wanna talk to you."

Lucy took a deep breath and started toward him. Better just to get it over with. They had to meet sooner or later.

"Hi, Billy. What happened with the police?"

He shrugged. "They got nothing on me. I wasn't down there. I never touched Abby."

Lucy pointed to the side. "Mind moving so I can get into my locker?"

"Uh, sure, no problem."

He jumped away, but then started to plead with Lucy. "Just listen for a second, okay, Lucy? I didn't hurt Abby. You know it too, because you stuck up for me."

"It's all right, Billy—I mean, it's cool."

"Lucy?"

"What?" she asked, becoming more impatient.

"Uh, could you get me in to see Abby?" he asked.

Lucy shook her head. "No."

"But—"

"It's only immediate family," Lucy replied.

"I said I was her cousin. Besides, after all the trouble you started—"

Billy's expression contorted into a beastly scowl. "Oh yeah, throw that in my face."

He stormed away from the locker before Lucy could say another word. She felt badly for Billy. Of course, there was always the possibility that he was the person who'd attacked Abby, but somehow, Lucy doubted it.

Lucy's fingers spun the combination on her locker door. She opened the locker and started to put her books inside. But then something fluttered out, dropping to the floor.

Lucy picked up a piece of watercolor paper. Someone had written an elaborate message on it, in calligraphy script.

I know who attacked Abby.

The last bell rang, startling Lucy. She immediately ripped up the message, thinking that it was the work of some sick joke. She dropped the pieces of torn paper into the garbage can at the end of the hall.

It was three o'clock. Time to see Abby.

Lucy caught the school bus that would drop her a block away from the hospital. It was strange being on the bus with all the juniors and sophomores. Cool kids never rode the school bus. Lucy had always gotten a ride with Abby.

Lucy intended to see Abby every day until she was able to leave the hospital. They had been best friends since kindergarten. Friends were supposed to stay loyal, she knew, especially in times of crisis.

After she left the bus, Lucy walked along Washington Street, crossing to the main entrance of the hospital. All the way up in the elevator, she kept imagining how Abby looked, all pale and bruised and lifeless. It made Lucy want to cry.

She entered the intensive care unit on tiptoes, moving slowly toward Abby's room. Lucy slipped into the doorway only to have her eyes grow wide and her jaw drop. She couldn't believe that Abby was sitting up in bed, grinning at her.

"Hi, Lucy!"

Lucy had to steady herself against the bed. "Abby, you look almost normal. You—but how?"

Abby kept smiling. "I feel fine," she replied. "A little headache, but otherwise I feel pretty good."

"Abby . . . ? Do you remember what happened to you? Can you tell the police who did this to you?"

Abby sighed. "The police have already been here. But I can't remember a thing. What happened to me?"

"You were attacked," Lucy replied.

Abby's brow fretted. "That's what Chief Danridge said."

Lucy shook her head. "Abby, how could you recover so quickly? Two days ago, you were in a coma!"

"The doctors seem to be amazed too," Abby replied. "But I don't have any memory of what happened. One minute I was at the homecoming game. The next minute I'm here."

"Abby, where's Billy's class ring? You had it around your neck at the game."

"I don't know," Abby replied. "I remember him giving it back to me, but I don't have it now."

Lucy knew the ring was the key to the mystery. If they found the person who had Billy's class ring, they would find the fiend who had hurt Abby.

Abby reached out for her best friend, touching Lucy's hand. "Hey, don't look so—"

Something shot through Abby's body. It was like a flash of light, or maybe a spirit pouring in and out of her. A burst of fear followed the lightning bolt. Suddenly, and for no good reason she could think of, Abby was afraid for Lucy.

"Don't go to school tomorrow," Abby said. "Don't, please—"

"It's all right," Lucy replied.

But Abby was starting to lose control. She had seen Lucy's death. It was as clear to her as the walls that surrounded them. Abby began to thrash wildly in the bed. Lucy backed away, totally freaked.

Lucy called for the nurse, who came running in with an intern. They restrained Abby while the intern filled a syringe with some yellow stuff. Abby felt the pinprick of the needle in her arm. The shot sent her back into the darkness.

Back where she couldn't warn Lucy.

Warn her to stay away from Central Academy.

Walking home from the hospital, Lucy felt terrible about Abby's condition. She was glad that her best friend had awakened, but there was something different about her. Why had Abby thrown that hissy fit in the hospital? Was there something wrong inside Abby's head? Had she suffered brain damage from the coma? Why would Abby insist that Lucy stay away from school?

Lucy shuddered, remembering the words of the calligraphy message. *I know who attacked Abby.*

Was there really someone at Central who knew the identity of Abby's attacker, or was the note simply the work of some wacko? Or maybe it was sent as a threat by the psychopath who had committed the awful crime.

The October wind whipped around Lucy's long neck, chilling her bones. Abby had seemed fine—until she lost it. What if the old Abby never came back?

Lucy hurried home to Prescott Estates. She tried to put the day behind her, but somehow she could not stop thinking about Abby.

Why did Abby warn her about school?

Not a minute after Lucy walked into the house the phone rang. Lucy flinched.

"Hello?" she said

For a moment there was silence and then heavy breathing.

"This isn't funny," Lucy said to the mysterious caller. "You sick creep!"

The reply crackled on the line. "Come to Central Academy and I'll tell you who attacked your friend Abby."

"What?"

"Come to Central. Now!"

Lucy's hands were trembling. "Who is this?"

"Come alone if you want to know the truth," the voice on the other end commanded.

"Who is this?"

Click.

"Hello? Hello?"

But the caller was gone, replaced by an impersonal dial tone.

Lucy hung up. She thought about calling

the police, but hesitated. The voice on the other end of the line had wanted her to go to Central Academy. Alone. It had to be a practical joke.

But maybe the strange caller *did* know who'd attacked Abby. Should Lucy be the one to receive that information? Why couldn't the caller go to the police?

Maybe it was someone who was afraid to come forward. Maybe the caller wanted Lucy to tell the police. As Abby's best friend, wouldn't she be the one to trust with the truth?

Lucy glanced at the phone. Shouldn't she call the police? The caller would probably run away if the authorities accompanied her to Central.

The phone rang again, making her jump.

"Hello?" Lucy said, grabbing the receiver.

"I'm waiting," the stranger said. "If you want to know who hurt Abby, be at your locker in thirty minutes."

"Who are you?" Lucy demanded.

"Don't worry, I won't hurt you."

Click.

Lucy hung up and looked at the clock. She could easily walk to Central in half an hour.

Be at your locker. . . .

How did the caller know Lucy's locker number? Was it someone she knew from school? One of the other girls from the cheerleading squad, perhaps, somebody who'd witnessed the attack but was scared to come forward?

I won't hurt you.

Lucy grabbed her sweater. She had to find out who had hurt her best friend.

The night was chilly and clear in Port City. Lucy could smell the ocean on the light breeze. Her legs felt weak and her stomach churned as she left Prescott Estates, turning onto Middle Road.

She barely remembered walking to the school as the Central Academy campus suddenly appeared in front of her. She hesitated at the end of Rockbury Lane, gazing toward the senior classroom building. Lucy had to go inside. She had to do it for Abby.

A side door had been opened on the north wall of the senior building. Lucy stepped into the archway, gazing down the dim hall. The interior of the school was completely silent—and dark. She groped on the wall for a light switch, but she didn't find one. The only light was from a dim "Exit" sign.

Her eyes scanned the black corridor again. "Hello? Are you there? I came, just like you said."

No reply.

It had been a trick. A horrible joke played by some mean-spirited sicko. And she had fallen for it.

"This isn't funny," she said, her voice echoing through the corridors of the school. "I'm leaving."

But as she started to turn, she heard the voice loud and clear. "You want to know who hurt Abby!"

Lucy glanced back over her shoulder.

"I tried to kill her!" the voice cried shrilly.

Lucy felt a cold rush of air and could sense, before she saw, someone coming toward her. Just as she turned, the club caught her squarely across the forehead. She tumbled backwards to the ground, banging against the hard walkway.

"I wish I'd killed Abby" the raspy voice croaked again. "But I guess you'll do for now."

Lucy tried to crawl forward but her head was throbbing. "No, please—"

The blunt object came down on the back of Lucy's skull. She began to tremble, twitching as the blood started to gush from her mouth and nose. She tried to raise herself up, but the third blow slammed her to the ground again.

"No—"

"Not dead yet?" the voice clamored.

A pool of crimson grew under Lucy's face as more blows rained down on her. She stopped breathing, though her muscles quivered involuntarily. From there on a sweet euphoria engulfed her, and she was at peace.

Lucy was suddenly free from her body. She saw a light that glowed in the distance. Two half-human shapes appeared out of the light and hovered before her.

"Hello, Lucy."

She heard the heavenly voices.

She also heard the murderer cackling over her body, but it already seemed so far away.

Lucy glanced through the rapidly closing door to the real world. Soon it would be closed to her forever.

She saw the class ring—Billy's class ring—being dropped in the pool of blood, spattering as it fell with a golden gleam.

ELEVEN

Abby stood at the huge picture window, gazing dolefully at the wet flakes of early November snow that fell from a dark sky onto the quiet streets of Port City. The winter storm had blown in overnight, covering the Wilder's front yard with a thick layer of white. Abby watched as the neighborhood children scurried along the sidewalk, scooping up cold handfuls to form ammunition for a snowball fight.

Abby turned away from the happy scene with tears in her eyes. It wasn't time for winter, not yet. She had missed most of the autumn as she lay in the hospital bed. Abby stumbled across the living room, flopping on the couch, crying, wishing that the dreary Sunday would go away.

Abby had been home for a week, recuperating in the comfort of her own bedroom. Her

parents had been wonderful to her. They had
attended her every need, hired a tutor to help
her catch up on the missed schoolwork from
Central Academy. Mrs. Wilder had taken some
vacation leave from her work to shuttle Abby
back and forth to the counsellor who had been
trying to help Abby deal with the tragedy that
had turned her life inside out. So far, things
hadn't really gotten much better.

A pain shot through the back of Abby's skull,
spreading toward her forehead. She winced,
grabbing her face. The headaches came and
went at random, sometimes lasting half an
hour. The spells were horrible, as if someone
had sliced into her head with an electric saw.
Abby hated taking the migraine pills that the
doctor had given her. The medication made
her depressed and drowsy.

The aching subsided mercifully, freeing
Abby from the pain. She wiped her teary
eyes, wondering if she would ever be rid of
the emotional and spiritual agony that had
gripped her. She could have dealt with everything else, the attack, the stay in the hospital.
She had no recollection of the attack, so except
for the physical pain, she didn't feel the weight
of that trauma.

Losing Lucy was another thing entirely.

Abby had never experienced a black void
like the emptiness that came with the death

of her best friend. Lucy's murder had devastated her. Abby had been waiting for Lucy to arrive during visiting hours when her mother came to tell her the bad news. It was almost as if her assailant had hit her again with the club. Abby had passed out, waking in fitful episodes, screaming for Lucy to come back.

"Abby, honey?"

She looked up to see her mother standing in the archway of the living room. Mrs. Wilder smiled at her daughter. Then she saw the frown on Abby's pretty face.

"Are you okay, Abby?"

Abby nodded. "Just another headache."

"Do you want me to get your pills?"

Abby shook her head. "It went away. But thanks anyway. I'll be all right."

"Are you sure?" her mother asked.

"Yes, Mom."

Mrs. Wilder sighed. "It's too early for winter, much too early." She could feel her daughter's pain, and wished it was her own. "Abby, some of the children knocked on the back door. They want to know if you'd like to help them build a snowman."

Abby smiled a little. "That's sweet. But I don't think so. Not today."

"Whatever you say, honey."

Mrs. Wilder started to turn back toward the kitchen.

"Mom?"

"Yes, Abby?"

Abby took a deep breath. "Uh, I was thinking about going out for a walk later."

Mrs. Wilder frowned. "I don't know, Abby."

There was great concern that the police hadn't caught the person who had attacked Abby and had doubtless killed Lucy. Chief Danridge was almost certain they were one and the same. It had been widely publicized that Abby had no memory of the episode, so the police hoped the killer wouldn't come after her since she could not make a positive identification. Still, they had warned Mr. and Mrs. Wilder to keep Abby at home as long as the killer was still on the loose.

"Please, Mom," Abby said. "Just a short walk. I won't go far. I haven't been outside since I got home."

"Don't you think it's better that you rest?" Mrs. Wilder said.

"That's all I've been doing," Abby said. "Resting! I'm all rested out. I need some exercise."

"Let's wait until your father gets home," her mother insisted. "Then he can walk with you."

Abby gave a defeated sigh. "All right."

Mrs. Wilder went back to the kitchen where she was busy preparing lunch for Abby.

Abby stood and walked back to the window. She kept thinking about Lucy. Abby hadn't been able to go to the funeral, hadn't even been to the grave yet.

The police still suspected Billy Major of foul play, though they'd come up with zero in the proof department. Billy had solid alibis for his whereabouts when the girls were attacked. However, his alibi had been Frankie Deets both times.

Could Billy and Frankie be in on it together? That sort of thing happened all the time, according to the headlines. Port City certainly wasn't immune to such violence. What if Billy had been the one to hurt them and Frankie was covering for him out of fear or for some other reason?

Abby shuddered. Would Billy come after *her*? The police had found his class ring next to Lucy's body, but that hadn't been enough for them to hold him for long. There was the chance someone was trying to pin the blame on Billy.

Her mother called from the kitchen. "Abby, lunch will be ready in a couple of minutes."

"Okay, Mom."

But Abby had no intention of sitting down to lunch. She slipped into the hallway, grabbing her coat and snow boots. She was determined to go for a walk. Ready for the snow and the cold, she eased out the front door, closing it gently so her mother wouldn't hear. She hurried along the sidewalk as fast as she could move on the snowy surface.

Abby knew where she was going—to Lucy's grave. To say goodbye to her best friend.

The cemetery was off Middle Road, fairly close to Prescott Estates. Abby strode along the walkways, past houses that were already adorned with Christmas lights. She hardly noticed them, thinking only of Lucy. Abby's eyes filled with tears. No swapping presents with her oldest and dearest friend this year— or any other year.

Abby reached the graveyard and asked the caretaker for directions to Lucy's headstone. Abby began to cry when she saw the name and date. It couldn't be! Lucy couldn't really be lying there beneath the white carpet. She had to be alive.

"Abby, over here!" a voice not unlike Lucy's said.

Abby lifted her head. Had she really heard her name? A cold wind whipped around her.

"Lucy! Please, come back."

A sudden warmth spread through Abby. She stood up straight. A weird sensation seemed to permeate every cell in her body. It was the same burst of spectral energy she had felt in the hospital, just before she had warned Lucy not to go back to school at Central. A spirit seemed to course through her own soul.

"Abby?"

Caught in a trance, Abby lifted her eyes to a glowing light that appeared before her. She saw the familiar face, recognized the lilt of the voice. Lucy was appearing to her in some kind of ghostly incarnation. There seemed to be another spirit with her, a smaller presence with a mischievous smile. Abby remembered her as well.

Abby wanted to speak but she couldn't utter a word. She just stood there, transfixed, frozen, dumbfounded. It was so eerie, yet somehow all too familiar.

"Abby," Lucy said, sounding far away, yet close by. "You have to help Billy."

Billy? Why did he need help? This couldn't be real. Abby wanted to believe this was some kind of hallucination, totally bogus.

But it wasn't. And Abby knew it.

"Billy will be hurt if you don't help him," Lucy said, her presence radiating a golden unearthly light. "You must help him."

Abby wanted to speak, to tell Lucy that Billy could've been the one who hurt both of them. But her lips would not move. She could only listen to her friend's voice.

"Help him, Abby. That's all I can tell you. I wasn't even supposed to come here, but my friend—"

Yes! Abby thought. *I remember the world*

beyond. I recall the shapes and lights of the other side.

"We'd better go," the small spirit seemed to say.

Lucy's shape started to fade. "Good-bye, Abby. I'll see you again, in a place that's more beautiful than you can imagine."

Abby's voice came back. "No! Lucy, please, I remember. I—"

A dizziness came over Abby. She saw black, and darkness overtook her. Her legs gave way and she fell to the ground, then felt nothing.

What felt like seconds later, Abby opened her eyes. Mrs. Seavey was standing over her, gently touching Abby's face.

"Abby, are you okay?" Mrs. Seavey inquired.

Abby remembered nothing of her vision. "Where am I?" she asked wildly.

"Lucy's grave," Mrs. Seavey replied. "I was coming here to put flowers on the plot. I miss her too, Abby."

Abby sat up. "How did I—"

"Shh, just relax," Mrs. Seavey urged. "I'll take you home. Does your mother know you're out here?"

"I—I don't know," Abby replied blankly.

Mrs. Seavey lifted Abby to her feet. Abby staggered a little as she walked toward the street. Her head was blank. Abby wouldn't remember anything until she saw Billy Major striding down the hallway at Central Academy.

Abby's first day back at school had been fairly uneventful. Everyone seemed glad to see her, though some of her old friends kept their distance. The entire student body was wondering the same thing—would the killer go after Abby again?

Abby went from class to class in a daze, barely comprehending anything. With the help of her tutor, she had been able to get up-to-date in most of her subjects. Her instructors were sympathetic. Mrs. Seavey had also intervened on Abby's behalf, urging the teachers to go easy on her.

Of course, the excruciating sense of loss was still with Abby. Lucy was not coming back. And it disturbed Abby that she had awakened at the grave with no memory of how she got there. All day long, she had been filled with a sense of urgency, as though there was something that she was forgetting.

But what?

As Abby left her fourth period class, she wandered through the crowded corridor, her head fuzzy. How was she going to get through life with all the pain and misery facing her every waking second? Would she ever recover from the trauma of Lucy's death?

"Abby?"

The voice had come from behind her. She turned to see Mrs. Seavey coming toward her. Abby was grateful to Mrs. Seavey for taking her home the day before. Her mother had given her a lot of grief about going out alone.

"Hi, Mrs. Seavey."

The fat woman smiled. "How are you doing?"

Abby shrugged. "Okay, I guess. I—" Abby's eyes widened and her mouth hung open.

"What is it, dear?" Mrs. Seavey asked.

Abby was staring at the swaggering form of Billy Major who strode down the hallway, coming straight toward her.

Abby heard the words in her head. *Help him.*

"It's all right," Mrs. Seavey said. "Don't—"

But Abby left her, heading for Billy. He stopped when he saw her coming. Abby went to him, putting her hand on his forearm.

"Abby!" Billy said dumbfoundedly. "What are you doing?"

She perceived Lucy over his shoulder, nodding at her. "Billy, you have to be careful."

Billy grimaced. "Everybody thinks I hurt you and killed Lucy. But I swear—"

"I know," Abby replied, cutting him off. "But you're in danger now, Billy."

"Me?"

Sweat had begun to pour from Abby's forehead. "Please, Billy, listen to me—"

"Look, Abby, there's a restraining order against me, and I have to stay away from you. Understand? If the cops see me—"

"Billy, please—"

He pulled away from her. "Sorry, babe, but you're gonna get me in trouble. I have to split. Later." Billy hurried away from her.

Abby followed Billy to the cafeteria, but he ran every time she attempted to get close to him. Try as she might, Abby was unable to escape the feeling that something bad would happen to Billy if she didn't prevent it.

But what could she do? Call the police? They wouldn't believe her. Abby couldn't do a thing, except wait and worry.

Billy Major stayed late after football practice. The regular season was over, but Central Academy still had two games left in the state playoffs. And the first game had been postponed a week because of the snowfall.

Billy decided to work on his weight lifting before the next playoff game. He liked to use the new machines in the weight room under the stadium. Lately, with all the strange things happening at Central, he needed to pump his muscles to relax.

What a lousy break, getting pegged for hurting Abby and killing Lucy. Billy knew he could never hurt anyone, let alone kill a person. But he was fairly sure that the cops were still tailing him whenever he moved around Port City. Billy had to wonder why the sorry Port City cops couldn't find the psycho mutant who had done all the damage.

Billy shifted from the fly machine to the bench press. He raised the bar upward, fixing the weights so he could slide beneath them for the upward movement. He'd put on thirty extra pounds, more than he had ever lifted. His arms felt strong today.

Sliding under the bar, Billy gripped the rough spots on the iron rod, taking a deep breath. He hoisted the bar just as the shadow appeared over him. He hadn't been expecting any company.

"Hey, what're you—"

Something hard struck the side of Billy's head, caving in part of his skull. He involuntarily released his grip on the weights, and the bar came crashing down on his throat, snapping his neck.

Billy saw a bright flash, and then his world turned white. He felt himself spinning toward the light. Somewhere the spinning stopped, and Lucy was there, waiting for him.

TWELVE

The funeral for Billy Major was held three days after his death. Abby attended the church service at the Old North Church in Market Square. The coffin was closed due to the disfiguring nature of Billy's "accident." Rumors were circulating that Billy had decapitated himself with the weight bar, and his death was anything but accidental.

Abby sat in the back row of pews, staring at the flowers that bordered the casket. She could not cry. There were no more tears inside her. Abby felt blank, suspended, as if nothing could possibly matter with her friends gone.

And Billy had been a friend. She'd forgiven him for getting rough with her, true. Yes, she had wished Billy would die, but not for real!

When the service ended, Abby hurried outside, crossing the street to hide behind a parked car. She watched as they loaded Billy into the black hearse. Abby could not bring herself to believe that Billy had killed himself. Nor could she believe Billy had been capable of hurting her and murdering Lucy.

After the hearse left for the cemetery, Abby moved slowly along the sidewalk, heading in the same direction of Billy Major's last ride. She wanted to take her time getting to the graveyard so everyone would be gone when she arrived there. Abby couldn't face Billy's family. Somehow, she felt responsible for Billy's death.

But who had killed Billy and Lucy? And why? What could her friends have done to make someone resort to murder?

It had to be a student at Central. Someone that Abby knew. Frankie Deets maybe?

Frankie was a dweeb, a whimpering coward. Of course, there could also be another side of Frankie, with some kind of evil lurking inside him. Abby knew from watching the six o'clock news that serial killers were often quiet, nerdy types who hid their savage instincts well.

Abby stopped at the Fife and Drum convenience store, purchasing a cup of hot chocolate. As she turned away from the counter, she saw the headline on the local newspaper: FOOTBALL HERO TO BE BURIED. And underneath:

MYSTERY OF CENTRAL STUDENT BODY DEATHS CONTINUES.

"Who?" Abby muttered to herself.

"I beg your pardon?" the counterman asked.

Abby shrugged. "Just talking to myself."

She spotted her reflection in the glass door of the shop. Her hair was flat and she had dark circles under her eyes. She wasn't pretty anymore. Not like she used to be.

Abby pushed through the door, stepping out onto the sidewalk again. She took tiny steps as she sipped the hot chocolate. Snow still lay on the ground and the sky overhead was darkening, ready to dump another load of white from the sky.

"Abby!"

She stopped for a moment, gazing toward the street. A blue car pulled up next to her. It was Mrs. Seavey, who rolled down her window to talk to Abby.

"Hi, Abby," she said in a kind tone. "What are you doing out here in the cold? It looks like snow again."

Abby sighed and nodded to the west. "I'm going to see Billy's—" She had to stop, choked by the words.

Mrs. Seavey took a deep breath. "Oh dear. I didn't realize you'd be taking it this hard."

"I know he hurt me," Abby replied. "But I didn't want him to die, Mrs. Seavey."

"They're saying he killed himself," Mrs. Seavey offered.

Abby did not reply.

"Well, get in," Mrs. Seavey said. "I'll take you over to the cemetery."

Abby shook her head. "No thanks."

"But this weather is—"

"It's all right, Mrs. Seavey," Abby replied curtly. "If I wanted to ride, I could take my own car."

She started away from Mrs. Seavey. Abby hadn't intended to be rude, she just wanted to do this her own way. She was tired of listening to everyone tell her how everything was going to be all right. It wasn't going to be all right, not if she couldn't bring her friends back.

Abby's timing was almost perfect. She arrived at the cemetery as the hearse pulled away from the front gates. A few people still lingered at the grave, so Abby had to wait awhile to be alone with Billy. Abby couldn't face him with an audience around.

Finally, the last mourner turned away from the headstone, leaving Billy to his final rest. Shadows were growing long as Abby stole into the graveyard, stepping between the markers to get to the fresh earth of Billy's grave.

The tombstone was clean and new like the marker on Lucy's grave. Were they both really gone? Abby had a flashing sense of someone standing before her.

She lifted her eyes to the shining shapes that seemed to poke through a tear in the sky. There were three of them this time. Lucy, the smaller spirit, and a boy.

Abby's jaw dropped. "Billy?"

"We can't stay long," Billy's apparition said.

Lucy shimmered with a heavenly glow. "We shouldn't even be here, Abby."

The small spirit seemed to giggle. "Breaking the rules again."

Abby's whole body jerked with a sudden bolt of energy. "I know!" she said slowly. "I remember. I—I was on the other side."

"We're on the other side now," Billy replied. "But we won't be coming back like you did, Abby."

"Who killed you?" Abby asked frantically.

"We don't know," Lucy replied.

Billy's voice was almost lifelike. "We couldn't tell you even if we knew."

"Then why have you come?" Abby demanded. "To torture me?"

"Be strong, Abby, " Lucy's spirit replied.

"We both loved you," Billy said. "We don't want to see you hurt. Be careful, Abby."

Abby grabbed her own hair, glaring angrily at the ghostly forms. "Tell me! Who did this? Who—"

Suddenly, the little spirit shot toward Abby, firing through her soul. Abby felt the rush of energy at the core of her being. Suddenly, she knew the identity of the murderer.

"I know—I see—I—"

Abby's eyes rolled back in her head. She slumped to the ground, losing it completely.

When she awakened from the blackout, Police Chief Victor Danridge was standing over her.

"What happened in the graveyard Abby?" Danridge asked.

Abby sat across from the policeman at the table. A steaming cup of hot chocolate sat in front of her. Danridge had brought her to the coffee shop after he found her at the cemetery.

Abby shrugged and sighed. "I don't know."

"You mean, you won't tell me. Is that it?"

She shook her head slightly. "No. I honestly don't remember."

She had no recollection of the spirits that had visited her. Had she remembered, Abby might have doubted her own sanity. For now, the past several hours had become a blank.

"Do you think Billy killed Lucy? And then himself?" Danridge asked bluntly.

Abby shook her head. "No."

Danridge leaned forward. "Abby, the day that Billy was found dead, you were seen earlier in the lunchroom trying to talk to him."

Abby frowned. She could not recall the day. Nor did she remember the visitations from Lucy. Something had wiped out the better part of her memory.

"Abby?"

"I just don't remember, Chief Danridge. It's like . . . I don't know . . . I just can't remember."

Danridge leaned back, exhaling. "I see."

"I'm sorry."

"Abby, I found you lying next to Billy's grave. What were you doing there?"

"I don't know."

Danridge took out his notepad and scribbled a few words. "Do you know anyone who would want to hurt Billy?"

"No."

"Not even yourself?"

Abby blushed. "I couldn't hurt him."

"What about the time he got rough with you and you kicked him in a rather painful place?"

She remembered that incident clearly, but Abby still had little recollection of today's events. "Yes, I did—but I didn't want to hurt him. I—"

"Take it easy," Danridge said in a calm tone. "I'm not accusing you of anything."

"I didn't *do* anything!" Abby insisted. "And I

keep having these—I don't know—these black-outs. I wake up and I don't remember a thing. It's horrible."

"You sustained a pretty bad blow to the head," Danridge said. "Maybe you should see your doctor."

"I will."

They were silent for a moment. Abby didn't feel threatened by Danridge anymore. She would have loved to answer his questions but she just couldn't.

"Abby, is there anyone you can think of, any-one at all, who could have done these things?"

She sighed. "I don't know."

"A student, a faculty member?"

Abby's face tensed as a name came to her mind. "Frankie. Yes, Frankie."

Danridge grimaced. "The Deets kid?"

"Yes," Abby replied tentatively. "I mean, he was hanging around with Billy all the time before Billy—"

She choked again on her words. Her memo-ry was muddled but she still recalled the worst of it. Billy and Lucy were dead. She could *nev-er* forget that.

"Deets, huh?" Danridge said skeptically. "He doesn't really seem the type."

Abby shuddered. "Frankie is a creep. I don't even know why Billy was hanging around with him."

"Maybe they were in on something together," Danridge offered. "That kind of thing happens all the time. Two guys, joking around, things get out of hand. The next thing you know—"

Abby shivered again. "Please, Mr. Danridge. Could I go home now?"

"I'd like to ask you a few more questions," the chief replied. "If you could—"

"The young lady said she would like to go home, Chief Danridge! Or didn't you hear her?"

They both looked up to see Mrs. Seavey standing a few feet away. She had a bag of take-out food in hand. Abby smiled, glad that her coach had arrived to rescue her from the policeman.

Danridge smiled. "Mrs. Seavey, I was just—"

Mrs. Seavey took a step forward. "How dare you treat a distraught young lady like this? Can't you see that Abby is upset? Why, if I hadn't stopped in here for my supper, you might've continued to hound her all night. She has rights, you know!"

Danridge looked at Abby. "I'm not holding you here against your will, Abby."

"Then I want to go," the blond-haired girl replied. "Mrs. Seavey, can you give me a ride?"

"Surely I will, Abby," she replied.

Abby started to get up.

Danridge stopped her. "I'll talk to the Deets kid, Abby. And if you remember anything that might be helpful to me, just call the station. I want to catch the person who did this to your friends."

Abby nodded. "All right."

She got up from the table, following Mrs. Seavey out of the coffee shop.

When they reached the street, Mrs. Seavey sighed. "The nerve of that man! Couldn't he see that you were upset?"

Abby smiled. "Thanks. I'll see you at school."

"Don't you want a ride?" Mrs. Seavey asked.

"I'll just walk."

Abby started off toward Prescott Estates, heading home.

"Phone me if you need anything," Mrs. Seavey called after her.

"I will," Abby said. "Thanks."

Darkness was starting to cover Port City, deep shadows falling over the streets. Abby felt a chill all over her body. She wanted to get home before the last ray of sunlight was gone.

A stiff wind began to blow in from the east, bringing damp air from the ocean. As Abby drew closer to home, she was filled with a sense of dread, as though something bad was going to happen. But when she arrived at the house, her mother and father were there, ready for dinner. They made a big fuss over Abby, asking where she had been and what she had been doing.

They ate dinner together, making small talk. Abby couldn't shake the sense of impending disaster. She began to wonder if someone was coming to kill her

She watched television for the rest of the evening, staying up even after her parents had gone to bed. It wasn't until she reached the eleven o'clock news that her fears were substantiated. The broadcast made her shriek and tremble. . . .

Frankie Deets had been found dead in his own bedroom. He had hanged himself. The police had found a suicide note, saying that Frankie had taken his own life out of guilt for killing Billy and Lucy.

The case, said Chief Danridge, was officially closed.

For now.

THIRTEEN

The days of winter dragged on with heavy snowfalls and record low temperatures. Abby stumbled through the bitter cold, numb inside and out, oblivious to the ravages of the harsh winter. The seasons did not exist for her. There was only the darkness, the sense of loss, the deep-set thorns of gloom and despair penetrating her heart.

Every school day, Abby wandered through the halls of Central Academy, unaware of the student body around her. At first they had stared and whispered at her, but now they just ignored the doleful creature who lived such a wretched existence.

Abby's parents paid close attention to their daughter, watching for signs of improvement. The counsellor told Abby that she would eventually get over her grief and depression. But

Abby did not believe him. She thought she would never shake the grim reality of her visits to the graveyard, once a day, to gaze down at the last resting places of her friends.

With each trip to the cemetery, Abby hoped that she would have one of the blackout episodes, so that she might try to remember something in the aftermath. But nothing ever happened, except for the wind whipping off the Tide Gate River, chilling her bones.

What had happened during those strange times when she had passed out? Hadn't she had some kind of bizarre experience in the hospital? Why did she think something would happen now?

Her memory did not serve her, even though the doctor had told her that the blows to her head had not caused any permanent brain damage. And her mind worked fine in her classes. Abby had managed to maintain a B + average, even with the unfortunate events that had destroyed her life.

Often Mrs. Seavey would show up at the graves herself, always bringing fresh flowers. The fat woman missed Lucy. And she regretted that she had suspected Billy when the real murderer was Frankie Deets.

Abby never challenged Mrs. Seavey. She had come to accept the fact that Frankie had killed

Billy and Lucy. Abby did not visit Frankie's grave.

She stayed in her funk until late April. But as spring came on, she felt the burden of sorrow lifting, as the counsellor had predicted. Abby didn't return to her old self right away, but the days became more bearable with the arrival of tulips, crocus, and daffodils.

Abby began to miss some of the old things that she had done before the tragedy. Then, on Easter Sunday, she dreamed that Lucy appeared to her, urging Abby to start cheer leading again. The next day, Abby asked Mrs. Seavey to put her back on the squad.

Mrs. Seavey, who had remained a loyal friend, reinstated Abby, as captain of the cheerleaders again. Mrs. Seavey was confident that, with Abby's return, Central had a chance to win the cheer-offs in the middle of May. The team began to practice hard, regaining some of the old spirit that had been present before Lucy's death.

Abby immersed herself in the acrobatics of the routines. The other girls were inspired to train harder when they saw Abby's dedication. Abby returned to her old form. The bags disappeared from under her eyes, the shine came back to her hair.

Mrs. Seavey kept encouraging Abby to be her best, to put the past behind her. Abby bought into the spirit of it, even if she did think that Mrs. Seavey was a walking cliché. The coach continued to help boost Abby back toward the smiling girl who had been the most popular senior at Central.

Abby's parents were pleased with their daughter's recovery. They invited Mrs. Seavey and the rest of the squad for a cookout on the first warm day of spring. The atmosphere was light and happy. There was much talk of the cheer-off in May. The contest was scheduled to take place at Rochester High.

At the party, Abby and the others did some cheers for Abby's parents. Mr. and Mrs. Wilder applauded, predicting victory. Abby beamed. It was the first time her parents had shown any real appreciation of her talents.

In a good-natured way, Mrs. Seavey warned the girls about being overconfident. They still had a lot of work to do. But if they persisted, she said, they had a good shot at the state championships.

After the party that night, Abby slept soundly, dreaming of Lucy. Lucy kept warning her to be careful. But Abby told her that everything was going to be all right.

She just knew it.

Mrs. Seavey stood in front of the cheer- leading squad, smiling at her girls. "Tomorrow is May fifteenth," she announced. "We've finally reached our date with destiny. The state cheer-off."

Some of the girls smiled weakly at Mrs. Seavey's overstuffed delivery. She was almost embarrassing with her clichés. But they knew deep down that Mrs. Seavey was right. Central Academy had a great chance to place first in the state competition.

"Our routines are sharp," Mrs. Seavey said. "You're all in perfect condition. And we have the best captain in the world."

Abby blushed a little. She had been working hard. It would be a big disappointment if Central didn't take home top honors.

"Now I want you all to get a good night's rest," Mrs. Seavey said. "The bus leaves first thing in the morning. Be here by seven o'clock."

Some of the girls groaned about the early hour.

"We want a chance to warm up after we get there," Mrs. Seavey urged. "It will give us an edge over the competition."

Abby spoke up. "Mrs. Seavey is right. Let's go for it and win!"

"That's the spirit, Abby," Mrs. Seavey said. "Now, I still don't have some of your parental consent forms. I hope you all have them."

"Mine's still in my locker," one girl said.

"Yeah," replied another, "I have to get mine

out of my notebook, but it's all signed."

"I left mine in my van," Abby offered.

Mrs. Seavey winked at Abby. "Okay, Abby, you get their forms and bring them to my office, okay?"

Abby nodded and set about the task of gathering the slips of paper that gave parental consent for the girls to compete in the cheer-off. She had to go all the way to the parking lot to get her own form. When everything was in hand, she returned to the girl's locker room under the stadium.

The lights in Mrs. Seavey's office were dark. Abby knocked on the door. No reply. Abby went in, turning on the lights.

Mrs. Seavey had not yet returned to her office. Abby went to her desk to leave the consent forms where the coach could find them. But when she went to drop the papers on top of the desk, one of them fluttered out, falling to the floor.

Abby had to go behind the desk to find the paper. She knelt down to pick it up. As she started to raise up again, something under the desk caught Abby's eye.

"A yearbook," she said to herself. "What's that doing down here on the floor? Mrs. Seavey must've dropped it."

Abby reached for the Central Academy yearbook from the previous year. The new one would be coming out in a couple of days. Abby straightened up, reaching to put the yearbook on top of the consent forms. But then she was seized by a sudden urge to look at the old junior pictures of her departed friends.

She smiled a little. "Lucy and Billy."

Thumbing open the pages, she looked for the smiling face of the dark-haired girl. "Hale . . . Lucy Hale." She reached the H's and scanned the page. There she saw something totally unexpected.

"Oh no! What—my God!"

Lucy's picture had a big black "X" over the face, as if she had been crossed out.

"No!"

She turned quickly to the M's to find Billy Major's picture. "Not him too!"

Billy's face had been exed out with the same crossed lines.

"Frankie Deets!"

Frankie had also been marked off.

Abby took a deep breath. She had to look in the W's for her own likeness. Her hands trembled as she turned the pages.

"No!"

Abby's junior picture had been crossed out.

She looked in the front of the book. A label had been pasted on the blank first page. PROPERTY OF MILDRED SEAVEY.

The office door swung open.

Mrs. Seavey started into the room. "Oh, Abby, I see that you've already—"

The fat woman froze when she saw Abby holding the yearbook.

"Abby, what are you doing?"

Abby's face had turned white. "I was just looking at the pictures of my friends."

Mrs. Seavey's eyes narrowed. "Then you know."

Abby dropped the yearbook on the desk and stepped back a little. "Uh . . . I don't know anything."

Mrs. Seavey slammed the office door behind her. "Don't play games with me."

"I just found this yearbook," Abby insisted. "Somebody crossed off the faces of—"

Abby hadn't seen the old mean expression on Mrs. Seavey's face for a long time. But there it was, that hateful glint in her eyes. Mrs. Seavey stepped forward slowly, picking up the yearbook.

"Such fools," the fat woman whispered.

Abby backed away from her, hitting the wall. There was no place to run, unless she went through Mrs. Seavey, who was much larger and stronger. Abby was trapped.

"Why?" she asked Mrs. Seavey. "Why did you do it?"

Mrs. Seavey glanced up, smiling sickly. "It was all for you, Abby. All for you."

Abby grimaced. "All for *me*? What did I—"

"Oh, I admit I attacked you first," Mrs. Seavey said. "I saw you waiting for him. That boy! You betrayed me, Abby. I thought you were going to stay away from him, devote yourself to the cheerleading squad. I loved you. I loved you like my own daughter. We could have had a special relationship, but you betrayed me."

Abby shook her head. "No, it couldn't have been you."

"It was! And now you know."

"What about Lucy?" Abby asked. "Why did you—"

"She knew," Mrs. Seavey replied. "She knew I was looking for you that night. If I let her live, she would've figured out that I was the one who attacked you."

Abby's heart pounded. She felt the pulse in her temples. Sweat broke out on her forehead. Could this really be true? Mrs. Seavey had killed her friends!

"What about Frankie?" Abby asked in a breathless whisper.

"He had to die," the fat woman replied. "He had to be sacrificed. If I made it look like he was the killer, then nobody would suspect me."

An expression of horror came over Abby's face. "Why?" she asked again. "Why?"

"For *you*," Mrs. Seavey repeated. "All for you. My Abby. You see, I had to kill my husband. He mistreated me. Once he knocked me down a flight of stairs and I got hurt so badly that I can never have children. I had to kill him. I made it look like an accident, though."

"But why for me?" Abby persisted. "I never asked for—"

"You were special!" Mrs. Seavey howled. "I loved you like my own child. More than your parents. We could've had a special life, Abby. You and me. Mother and daughter. Forever."

Abby shook her head. "You're not my mother, Mrs. Seavey. You never will be."

A calm look came into Mrs. Seavey's eyes. "No, not now. Because I have to kill you."

Abby's entire body trembled as the fat woman inched closer. "Please, Mrs. Seavey. You need help."

Mrs. Seavey pushed Abby against the wall, looking into her eyes. "My daughter."

"No, I—"

The fat woman touched Abby's hair, stroking the tresses with a loving hand. "My own Abby. My daughter. My life. My reason for living. My beautiful daughter."

"Please, Mrs. Seavey, turn yourself in—"

But the fat woman only embraced Abby. "I have to kill you, darling. You know I do."

Abby started to say something, but she saw

movement over Mrs. Seavey's shoulder.

Three lights had begun to glow in the office.

The spirits had appeared again.

Lucy!

Billy!

And the smaller bundle of giggling light.

"I loved you, Abby," Mrs. Seavey muttered. "I don't want to kill you. I must, though. I must."

But Abby was no longer listening to the madwoman. She had her eyes trained on the spirits. Abby was sure that her departed friends had returned to help her.

FOURTEEN

Abby kept gazing at the three ethereal beings that hovered over Mrs. Seavey's head. "Lucy, Billy," she whispered.

"Yes," Mrs. Seavey replied, thinking that Abby was talking to her. "I had to get rid of them. They weren't any good for you, Abby. They only brought you down."

Lucy spoke from above. "Don't let on that you can see us, Abby. Mrs. Seavey doesn't know we're here."

"Can you help me?" Abby asked.

Mrs. Seavey replied, "I probably could. But you'd have to keep your mouth shut. You must never tell anyone what I did to those kids. Is that clear?"

"Don't listen to her, Abby," Billy said. "She's strong. She killed us so she could kill you."

Abby hesitated with Mrs. Seavey still holding her in a tight embrace. Was she really hearing the voices of her friends? Or was it some cruel hallucination brought on by fear?

The smaller spirit smiled down at Abby. "We can help you now that you know who the killer is."

"I thought you weren't supposed to interfere," Abby whispered.

The three of them replied in unison, "We're not."

Mrs. Seavey drew back. "What are you talking about?"

Abby blushed. "Uh, nothing."

Mrs. Seavey smiled and touched Abby's cheek. "Could you keep this to yourself, Abby?"

Lucy's image seemed to pulsate with a weird energy. "Agree with her, Abby. Tell her anything."

"Uh, sure, Mrs. Seavey," Abby replied. "I could—"

Something crackled next to the other spirits. A fourth being glowed into life. It took a moment to form, but Abby immediately recognized the shape of Frankie Deets.

"Whoa," Frankie's ghost remarked. "This is radical. How did I—look, it's Abby!"

His name formed on Abby's lips. "Frankie."

Mrs. Seavey emitted a plaintive sigh. "Yes, he was difficult. I waited until after the police questioned him. Then I sneaked into his house to kill him. He really struggled—"

"You're darn right I did!" Frankie's spirit replied. "Watch her, Abby! She's stronger than she looks."

Mrs. Seavey's voice droned on. "I didn't want to do it to those kids, Abby. But I had to. They were no good for you. My own little Abby, the daughter I never had."

"She's a sicko," Frankie offered.

"I don't hate her for killing us though," Billy remarked.

"We can't hate her," Lucy said. "Not here. But we can help you Abby, even if it is against the rules."

Mrs. Seavey turned her head back, gazing in the direction of the spirits that she could not see. "What are you looking at, Abby? Huh? Tell me!"

"Keep humoring her!" Frankie warned. "You can fool her, Abby!"

Lucy sounded distraught. "What are we going to do?"

Billy glanced at the little spirit. "Is there any way we can help Abby?"

The smaller ball of light crackled and flickered. "We must hurry. We don't have much time, not in this dimension."

"What are you looking at?" Mrs. Seavey demanded. "Look at *me*, Abby! I'm the one who cares for you. Not your mother and father. You're *my* daughter. Do you understand?"

Abby lowered her eyes to meet the gaze of the madwoman. Mrs. Seavey's face burned with hatred. Abby tensed, fearing for her life, ready to move. She had to fight back. She wasn't going to die like her friends.

The spirits flickered, as if they could read every thought in Abby's confused head.

"Don't fight her, not yet!" Frankie warned.

Billy was spinning in a circle. "No, Abs, don't do it. Not yet, wait for us."

"She's going to stand up to Mrs. Seavey," Lucy said. "Don't do it, Abby."

The little spirit still seemed calm. "She must do what is necessary."

"What can we do?" Lucy asked.

"*We* must do what is necessary," the little being replied.

Mrs. Seavey grabbed Abby and shook her. "What are you looking at, Abby? Are you crazy?"

Tears welled in Abby's eyes. For the first time in months, she was able to cry. The salty pearls streaked down her face. She stared straight into Mrs. Seavey's wicked eyes.

"What's wrong with you?" the fat woman demanded.

Abby suddenly blurted out the truth. "I'm looking at my friends!" she cried. "The ones you killed!"

Mrs. Seavey laughed.

Abby felt her own strength growing. "The three of them," she said. "Lucy, Billy, and Frankie. And they're with my friend, a being I knew on the other side. I was there, Mrs. Seavey, after you hurt me. I was in another dimension."

"Dear child, you've gone insane," Mrs. Seavey replied.

"They're here!" Abby insisted. "Just look!"

"She's going to do it!" Frankie said.

Lucy crackled and sparked. "No, Abby."

"She has to," Billy rejoined.

"It must be," the little spirit offered.

Abby nodded over Mrs. Seavey's shoulder. "Just look. They can see you. They know what you did, Mrs. Seavey!"

Mrs. Seavey turned reflexively to look up at the ceiling. "There aren't any—uh—"

Abby gave her a shove, sending the fat woman sprawling across the desk. She was free for a moment. Abby darted toward the glass door of the office, reaching for the knob. But Mrs. Seavey was quick. She recovered her balance in time to make a leap for the blond-haired girl. Abby felt the strong, fat hands closing on her shoulders.

"You're going to tell!" Mrs. Seavey cried. "You're going to get me in trouble!"

Abby wheeled around, slapping Mrs. Seavey's face hard.

"Good one, Abs!" Billy cried.

"Hit her again," Frankie insisted.

"Give her one for me," Lucy rejoined.

The little spirit only watched serenely as its aura glowed about it.

Mrs. Seavey gave a horrid cry. She shifted her massive weight, flinging Abby across the room. Abby crashed into a filing cabinet, bouncing off to hit the floor.

"She's in trouble," Billy said.

"No!" Frankie replied. "Mrs. Seavey will kill her!"

"Can't we do something?" Lucy asked the little spirit.

Mrs. Seavey loomed over Abby as she tried to rise from the floor. "You're no better than the rest," Mrs. Seavey railed. "I wish I had killed you the first time. It would have made things so much easier."

Abby struggled to her knees, lifting her arms to fend off the attack from the large woman. Mrs. Seavey began to beat her with clenched fists, kicking her with the hard toe of her shoes. The madwoman kept muttering about how she would get rid of the body. How

Abby would never be seen again.

Abby tried to fight back, but she was stunned and weak. Mrs. Seavey's hand closed around an aluminum softball bat that was leaning against the wall. She lifted the bat, holding it over her head.

"I'm sorry I have to kill you, Abby. You could have been so special to me. You could've been. . . . What the—"

Suddenly the office was filled by a blinding light. Mrs. Seavey had to cover her eyes with her hands. She dropped the softball bat in front of Abby.

Abby also saw the heavenly flash. The four spirits above her had combined into one big ball. The ball was spinning like a pinwheel as it came toward Abby.

The light ball entered Abby's body, coursing through the core of her being. She felt herself lifting from the floor. When she got to her feet, she gazed toward Mrs. Seavey who gaped at her.

"You can't hurt me now," Abby said.

Mrs. Seavey squinted her eyes. "What? I—"

Abby stood her ground. "Give up, Mrs. Seavey."

But the fat woman was not ready to surrender. She reached down, picking up the softball bat. Again, she brandished the aluminum bat.

"You were never any good!" Mrs. Seavey cried. "Never!"

She started to swing the bat at Abby's head.

But Abby's body was filled with a ghostly burst of energy. She shot forward, crashing into the fat woman. This time Mrs. Seavey flew across the room, smashing against the wall. She lay there, stunned for the moment.

The spirits flew out of Abby's body. They circled in the pinwheel until they were able to separate. Then they gazed down at Abby from the ceiling again.

"Run," the little spirit said.

Abby hurried out of the office with the four spirits on her tail. She left the locker room, running through the dark corridor under the stadium. When she reached the open spaces of the Central campus, she hesitated, wondering where to flee. It was getting late. Everyone had already gone home for the day.

"I have to get home," Abby said. "My mom and dad will help me. I have to call the police."

But the little spirit was there in front of her, shining in Abby's eyes. "You cannot escape her, Abby. She has things that will make you look like the killer. You have to face her. We will help as much as we can."

Abby's body trembled. "But I—"

"Listen to her," Lucy urged.

"Don't end up like us," Billy rejoined.

"Face the darkness," the smaller spirit said. "You are the light, Abby."

Face the darkness.

Abby wanted to flee, but something held her back. Then she heard the voice of Mrs. Seavey, loud and threatening, echoing in the corridor. She was coming after Abby.

Face the darkness.

Abby regarded the small sprite in front of her. "Where?" she asked. "Where do I go?"

"I can tell you no more!" the spirit replied.

"I don't want her to hurt me," Abby said. "If I face the darkness will I—"

"I can tell you no more!"

Mrs. Seavey's footsteps were audible in the cool night air. She was getting closer. Abby had to do something.

Face the darkness.

She glanced toward her departed friends, but their images were starting to fade. Suddenly Abby was alone. And the madwoman shuffled through the long tunnel, coming after her like a zombie from some horror movie.

"Face the darkness," Abby said to herself.

She had to fight Mrs. Seavey. But how? Where could she run? The Central campus sprawled before her.

Abby heard the voices floating on the air.

"Run for the gym, Abby."

"You can stop her, Abs."

Mrs. Seavey bellowed behind her.

Abby turned toward the Central gymnasium, running pell-mell through the lengthening shadows of spring.

FIFTEEN

Abby bolted through a side door that had been left open on the north corner of the gymnasium. It was pitch black inside the huge, open structure. Abby called out for help, hoping that one of the coaches had stayed late. But there was no answer, except the cool breeze that rushed past Abby's face.

Where would she hide in the darkness? How could she escape the half-mad Mrs. Seavey? If only she hadn't listened to the spirits, which were probably hallucinations anyway, brought on by the wound to her head.

"I'm coming for you, Abby!" Mrs. Seavey called from outside. "I know where to find you!"

Abby turned in a circle. There was nowhere to run, no place that she could see anyway.

She took a step back toward the door but Mrs. Seavey's shadow had appeared there at the entrance.

"Abby! This is your last chance. We could be special friends if you'd just see things my way."

Abby froze in the middle of the gym floor. What was she going to do? Let Mrs. Seavey kill her?

"Abby, over here!"

She heard the buzzing of an ethereal voice. The call had simply appeared in her head. Abby turned sideways to see a dim light glowing under the bleachers.

"Abby, come quickly."

Real or imagined, one of the spirits was showing her the way to a hiding place. Abby darted across the floor toward the light. One section of bleachers had been opened for a faculty assembly. Abby slipped through the tiered rows and lowered her thin body down into the metal understructure of the bleachers.

Abby sat motionless, watching the frame of the entrance. A warmth engulfed her, a glowing life-force. She knew that Lucy's soul had wrapped around her.

"It's wonderful," Lucy said. "I've never known such happiness. But it's not your time, Abby."

"Lucy, are you real or what?"

The warmth disappeared, leaving Abby to lean back against the cold metal of the bleacher structure.

Mrs. Seavey staggered through the doorway. A flashlight beam sliced into the darkness. Abby closed her eyes when the bright ray burned into her pupils. Had Mrs. Seavey seen her?

"Abby, we can be friends. You don't have to be afraid of me. We can talk it out."

Abby opened her eyes to see the flashlight coming toward her. She prayed that Mrs. Seavey hadn't seen her under the bleachers. But the fat woman strode up the tiers, climbing to hover right over Abby's hiding place.

"I see you, you little rat!" Mrs. Seavey called.

Abby held her breath. Something crashed on the bleacher seats above her head, startling her. Mrs. Seavey was using the aluminum baseball bat to smash the wooden surface.

"I'll get to you, little rat!" the madwoman said. "I'll flush you out of your hole."

Abby flinched each time the bat came down on the bleachers. The entire structure shook and rattled. But then the pounding stopped and Abby lifted her head to look into the flashlight.

"There you are," Mrs. Seavey said.

A hand came through the bleachers, closing

around Abby's wrist. Abby screamed and drew back further into the iron mesh of the underside. Mrs. Seavey couldn't reach her after she had retreated.

"You'll never get me now!" Abby cried. "You can't fit under here!"

The aluminum bat crashed again.

Abby flinched.

But then she heard Mrs. Seavey stomping back to the gym floor. For a moment, Abby thought she was safe. At least until she heard the dull rattling in front of her.

"I can't get you, eh?" Mrs. Seavey railed. "Well, what's to stop me from crushing you in this section of bleachers? Huh, little rat? It's going to be easy to kill you."

What's she going to do? Abby wondered.

Abby felt the vibrations that shot through the steel network as the bleachers started to move. She realized with horror that Mrs. Seavey was going to close the entire section, trapping Abby and mangling her in the bargain. The space under the seats began to grow smaller.

How was she going to escape this time?

"Abby, climb!"

She lifted her eyes to see Lucy's light glowing above her.

"Climb through the bleachers and go upward, Abby!"

Frankie Deets's ghost was behind her, drifting through the bleachers, pointing the way.

"She can't follow you up there," Billy called from the highest rafters of the gymnasium.

"They're going to get me killed," Abby muttered, wondering if she'd be joining her friends sooner than expected.

But she climbed anyway, barely squeezing through the bleachers as Mrs. Seavey pushed them forward.

The flashlight shined in her eyes. "There you are!" Mrs. Seavey smashed the aluminum bat on the seats.

"Climb, Abby," Lucy's voice urged. "She can't get you if you go up."

Abby's feet and legs pumped as she ran the bleachers to the top row. She could hear Mrs. Seavey behind her. The fat woman's weight made a horrible racket on the trembling tiers.

"Won't escape me!" she cried. "I'll have to kill you now, Abby. You ruined it!"

When Abby reached the top of the bleachers, she glanced to both sides only to see that the other tiers of bleachers had been pushed into the wall. One narrow line of flat wood spanned the entire length of the gym. There was no way down unless she dropped thirty feet or went through Mrs. Seavey.

The bat hit wood again. "You can't run, Abby. There's no place for you to escape me."

"Here, Abby!"

She glanced toward the far end of the gymnasium. Lucy's ethereal form glowed there. Billy, Frankie, and the small spirit were also flying high, circling behind Lucy.

"Come to us," they said in unison.

Abby hesitated, listening as Mrs. Seavey drew closer.

"Hurry, Abby," Lucy's spirit told her.

With catlike agility, Abby ran across the narrow beam of wood. She knew Mrs. Seavey was behind her. She could feel the vibrations. But Mrs. Seavey wasn't as fast as Abby.

"Here!" Lucy said. "Come here, Abby!"

Abby had reached the end of the bleachers. She gazed toward the steel rafters of the ceiling structure. There was no place left to go. The spirits had led her astray.

"Here, Abby," Lucy beckoned from the rafters. "You can do it."

"Yes," Frankie rejoined. "She can't get you here."

"Hurry," Billy told her.

Abby squinted at the steel girder that had to be at least ten feet away. "I can't make it."

"Jump!" Lucy told her.

Mrs. Seavey slammed the bat against the wall. "I'm here. And this time I'm really going to kill you!"

She was almost on top of Abby.

"Jump!" the spirits said in unison.

The aluminium club was only inches away as it crashed into the wall next to Abby's head.

"Now you die!" Mrs. Seavey cried.

Abby had no choice. She tensed, anticipating the heavy impact of the bat. But instead of facing the blow, Abby leapt out into the darkness, diving for the cold steel of the ceiling beam.

"No!" the fat woman bellowed.

Abby's stomach turned as she sailed through the air. She could see the girder in front of her. She caught the edge and held on tightly, swinging back and forth. For a moment, she thought she was going to lose her grip on the narrow rim of iron.

"Damn your eyes!" Mrs. Seavey cried. "Just fall and make my life easier!"

Abby's fingers suddenly felt sweaty.

"You can't hold on, Abby!" Mrs. Seavey bellowed.

Lucy was right there, her aura shining like a halo. "Don't listen to her, Abby. Swing up, the way we did on the monkey bars when we were kids."

Abby swung her legs upward, catching the girder, wrapping around the beam. She righted herself, balancing there until she caught her breath. Lucy had been right. Mrs. Seavey couldn't reach her now.

The flashlight beam swung over Abby. "There you are."

"You can't hurt me now," Abby said. "I'll stay here until morning. Somebody will come."

But Mrs. Seavey was no longer listening. She rumbled across the bleachers, heading for the open tiers. She was obviously on her way down. What did she have up her sleeve now?

Another light glowed across the gym, hovering in the rafters. Why had the spirits chosen to congregate on the opposite side of the dark building? Did they really want Abby to walk all the way across the steel beams? They were narrow and treacherous.

"Abby, come here!"

"No," Abby cried. "I'll wait here. She can't get me. She's leaving. I'm safe."

"No, you're not," Lucy called.

"There's a door over here," Frankie said.

"She's coming, Abby," Billy added. "She's on the way. She can climb up from the outside. And she has a key."

Lucy urged her to start moving. "Abby, you have to get to the door before Mrs. Seavey. Otherwise, she'll come out after you."

Abby was trembling. Sweat had broken out over her body. How was she going to walk all the way across the ceiling rafters? Yet, she had to make it if she was going to escape Mrs. Seavey.

"Why are you doing this to me?" Abby called.

But the spirits were no longer there.

Abby had to do it alone.

She gradually rose to her feet, finding her balance on the narrow rafter. Groping in the darkness, she found the crosspieces that spanned the area above her. Using the crosspiece as a safety rail, she started forward, taking a few inches at a time.

"Hurry," a voice said from nowhere.

Abby tried to move faster, but it was slow going in the shadows. Still, she managed to make some headway, moving gradually toward the catwalk in the distance. If she could just make the observation platform and the access door, she would be able to get away from Mrs. Seavey.

As Abby gained confidence, she started to step a little faster. When she was almost halfway across the gym, she stopped for a moment to look down into the dark pit. Her head spun a little. She snapped her eyes forward, closing them until the vertigo subsided.

"Steady," she told herself.

"Hurry," the voice said from the shadows.

Abby stepped onto a narrow girder. Her foot hit a round-headed rivet with a polished surface. The sole of her sneaker slipped across the rivet. Abby fell, catching the rafter below her with one hand. She dangled there, about to plummet into the darkness below.

Using her other hand, she grabbed the rafter and swung up again. Her body was weak, shaking with fear. And she was still a good twenty feet from the catwalk.

The spirits glowed before her.

"You have to make it, Abby," Lucy's voice urged.

"Hurry," said Frankie Deets.

Billy seemed to be waving. "Come on, Abby. You can do it."

With the help of her departed friends, Abby started forward again in the darkness. She had to step much slower, feeling the way with the bottoms of her feet. The catwalk was getting closer. In a few more minutes, she'd be able to step over the railing onto the narrow platform where they filmed all the basketball games at Central.

"You're almost there, Abby," Lucy told her.

Billy was vibrating like a candle flame. "Come on, Abs."

Frankie gave his encouragement. "That's it, Wilder."

But the younger spirit replied, "We cannot stay much longer."

Abby inched her way toward the railing. It was barely out of reach. She stretched her arm once, almost touching the thin steel of the catwalk.

A few more steps. She reached again. The cold steel sent a chill through her fingers.

Abby grabbed the railing and swung onto the catwalk. But as soon as she had landed, the door at the other end swung open. Mrs. Seavey entered from outside, standing on the catwalk, blocking Abby's exit. There was no place for the blond-haired girl to go except back on the rafters.

Mrs. Seavey slammed the softball bat into the railing. "It's over, Abby. You know, you never could do that pyramid very well!"

Abby started over the railing to climb back onto the rafters where Mrs. Seavey couldn't follow her. Mrs. Seavey slammed the bat against the railing again. When it vibrated, Abby lost her grip. She tumbled off the catwalk, grabbing the edge of the girder as she fell. Abby dangled from the rafters with nothing but the gym floor to stop her if she lost her grip.

The catwalk trembled as Mrs. Seavey came toward her. "Well, well. Look who's hanging around the gym. Ha! I made a funny."

"No!" Abby cried.

Mrs. Seavey raised the bat over her head. "Let's make this short and sweet, Abby. I'll drop you and then tell everyone how I tried to keep you from committing suicide. It'll be a tragic story indeed."

Abby closed her eyes. But then she sensed a warmth all around her. As Mrs. Seavey swung the ball bat toward Abby's defenseless hands, an unearthly force invaded Abby's lithe body.

Abby felt herself being propelled upward, swinging through the darkness. When Abby came over the railing, her feet landed in Mrs. Seavey's chest. Mrs. Seavey tumbled backward, going over the thin barrier of iron. Abby tried to grab her, but it was too late. Mrs. Seavey screamed. Her body sent a thunderous echo through the gym when it smashed on the floor below.

Abby stood there, looking down into the shadows. She could not see the lifeless form. But she knew Mrs. Seavey was dead.

The lights glowed in front of Abby for a moment. She wanted to ask Lucy something, but the aura dimmed quickly. The spirits had helped her but they were gone now. Abby could only wonder if Mrs. Seavey had joined them in the joyous world beyond matter.

After a while, Abby climbed down the outside ladder to call the police.

She was taken into custody, and kept at the juvenile detention center until they sorted out the truth. It took all day and all night for them to believe her story about Mrs. Seavey. Abby left out the part about the spirits of her dead friends.

She knew that no one would believe her anyway.

EPILOGUE

On Graduation Day, the sun rose over Port City, filling a cloudless June sky. Abby's mother called her from downstairs, making sure that Abby was out of bed. Abby had been awake for nearly an hour, lying under the sheets, wishing that she could somehow cancel the ceremony that had been scheduled for later that morning.

"We don't want to be late," Mrs. Wilder called. "And you want to look your best, dear. This is one of the most important days of your life, Abby."

Abby just groaned and looked up at the ceiling. Graduation Day had come too soon for her. The tragedy and loss of the recent months was still with her. She had been going to counselling twice a week, but the grim reality of death and betrayal loomed large in the young woman's life. Would she ever be able to forget what had happened? And if she couldn't forget, would she ever learn to at least live with the trauma?

Mrs. Wilder appeared at Abby's bedroom door. "Rise and shine, sleepyhead. You don't want to miss your graduation."

"Yes, I do," Abby replied.

"Honey, this only happens once in your life, at least for high school. You don't want to miss it."

Abby sighed. "What difference does it make? Lucy won't be there. Neither will Billy."

Mrs. Wilder patted her daughter's shoulder. "Who knows? Maybe they will be there. You can't really tell."

Abby shuddered. She remembered all too well the visitations by the spirits of her departed friends. Had they been real or just manifestations of her imagination? Either way, the spirits had played a big part in her survival.

Mrs. Wilder gazed at her daughter with a concerned expression. "Well, if you really don't want to go—"

"No," Abby replied quickly. "You're right, Mom. I owe it to Billy and Lucy to go. Even Frankie."

"You miss them, don't you? It must be horrible. I never lost a close friend like that."

Abby threw back the sheets. "I better get ready."

When she was showered, brushed, and dressed, Abby went downstairs to have breakfast with her parents. Mr. Wilder looked up from the morning paper when she walked into the kitchen. Abby flopped down in a chair and stared blankly at her eggs and toast.

"Morning, Princess," her father said.

Abby sighed. "Yeah, I guess."

Mr. and Mrs. Wilder exchanged a furtive look.

"Uh, I picked up a course catalogue from the community college, Abby," Mr. Wilder offered. "I figured since you haven't applied to any of the state schools, you could look over the local campus."

Abby shrugged. "Okay."

Her parents were worried that she hadn't shown much interest in attending college.

"Port City Community isn't a bad school," Mrs. Wilder offered. "You could transfer after two years."

"Sure," Abby replied. "Why not?"

After breakfast, they all went outside to get into the car. It was a glorious summer day, bright and breezy. Abby looked up at the blue sky.

"Let's walk to Central," she said suddenly. "Please?"

Mr. Wilder shrugged and looked at his wife. "Okay. It is a beautiful day. I think the walk would do us good."

The three of them started along the sidewalk, heading for the school. As Abby drew closer to Central Academy, she began to feel a sense of elation, a happiness that had been absent for a long time. The feeling grew as she marched in the processional, clad in her red gown and mortarboard.

They're here, she said to herself. Lucy, Billy, Frankie. I can feel them. They want me to graduate. They're watching me from the other side.

One by one, the matriculating students filed past the lectern, receiving their diplomas from the principal of Central Academy. When Abby took her diploma from the principal's hand, the student body erupted with applause. They gave her an unexpected standing ovation that brought tears to Abby's eyes.

She lifted her gaze to the sky. For a moment, she thought she saw four bundles of light looking down at her. But then she realized it was only the reflection of the sunlight glistening through her tears.